AF338594

The Case of
The Beggars' Coppice
An Edda Case Mystery

By
Erica Lawson

Also by Erica Lawson

Possessing Morgan
The Chronicles of Ratha: Book 2 Lion Among the Lambs
The Chronicles of Ratha: Book 1 Children of the Noorthi
Out of Retirement
Miss-Match
Reflected Passion
Soulwalker

The Case of
The Beggars' Coppice
An Edda Case Mystery

by
Erica Lawson

Affinity
eBook Press
NZ
2015

The Case of The Beggars' Coppice
An Edda Case Mystery

© by Erica Lawson 2015

Affinity E-Book Press NZ LTD
Canterbury, New Zealand

1st Edition: ISBN: 978-1-98-858818-6

All rights reserved.

No part of this e-Book may be reproduced in any form without the express permission of the author and publisher. Please note that piracy of copyrighted materials violate the author's rights and is Illegal.

This is a work of fiction. Names, character, places, and incidents are the product of the author's imagination or are used fictitiously and any resemblance to actual persons living or dead, businesses, companies, events, or locales is entirely coincidental

Editor: Ruth Stanley
Proof Editor: Alexis Smith
Cover Design: Irish Dragon Designs

Acknowledgments

To my family, I thank them for their support over what has been a difficult year.

To Affinity, my thanks for letting me write at my own pace and allowing me the space to find my mojo again.

Dedication

To AF

Table of Contents

Chapter One 1
Chapter Two... 10
Chapter Three.. 18
Chapter Four 33
Chapter Five.. 43
Chapter Six... 56
Chapter Seven 71
Chapter Eight 86
Chapter Nine 96
Chapter Ten... 107
Chapter Eleven.. 120
Chapter Twelve.. 135
Chapter Thirteen 145
Chapter Fourteen... 159
Chapter Fifteen... 168
Chapter Sixteen.. 177
Chapter Seventeen... 185
Chapter Eighteen... 196
Chapter Nineteen... 213
Chapter Twenty.. 223
About the Author 231
Other Books from Affinity eBook Press................... 233

Chapter One

Edda Case stood in the snow-covered cemetery looking down into the three-by-eight-foot hole at her feet. Today was not a day for joy, but for sorrow, and the falling snow reflected her tears.

"Ashes to ashes…dust to dust…" The priest's low tone expressed the solemnity of the occasion and did little to comfort Edda's broken heart.

She looked down at the single rose in her gloved hand and allowed it to slip from her fingers and onto the coffin. "Goodbye, Junee-moon." The words tasted like dust on her tongue. She'd had months to prepare for this day, but it was still a day that had come too soon.

Edda walked away from the grave before anyone could approach her. June's death was a wound too open to face mourners. They would all say how sorry they were, that June had died too soon, and that she was holding up well after that insidious disease had taken her partner. She didn't want to hear all that. She had told herself all this, and more, in the days leading up to, and after, June's passing.

She left immediately after the burial and drove home. If she had stayed, there would have been the curious and well-wishers among the mourners wanting to chat. Edda didn't want to even try to socialize. She just wanted to be left alone in her sorrow.

The snow lay thick across the footpath leading to her apartment building, blocking her way until she kicked it aside. When she opened her apartment door there was a lone lamp inside to guide her way and she was content with its ambient glow.

Edda slumped on the sofa and sat there, not even bothering to remove her snow-laden coat. The ticking of the wall clock roared in her ears as it broke the silence of the room. She could feel the loneliness already, crawling inside her and inhabiting her soul. This time she didn't stop herself, and her grief overwhelmed her. Her sobbing became a howl, screaming at the injustice of death taking the one person who had ever truly meant something to her. Her fists pounded the cushions beside her and her body slumped further until she was lying down. She had no fight left to get up and go to bed.

She closed her eyes and tried to block out the world, even if it was only for a short while. For a fleeting second Edda considered joining June. Nothing appealed to her anymore, so why prolong the pain? But she knew better. June would slap her for even considering such a thing.

Something brushed her skin and she jumped. She heard a pitiful meow and she grabbed what she knew was sitting inches away from her face. "Jasper," she whispered. Edda buried her face in his fur and cried, not caring in the least that she was using the cat as a tissue. The cat cried again and tried to escape, but Edda valiantly held on until the cat became belligerent.

Edda could feel the wisps of cat fur on her face, fluttering when she breathed. She giggled and sat up, but the pain in her heart destroyed whatever laughter she could muster. Her hand rose to her hair and combed through her short auburn locks, finally resting on the back of her neck. What was she going to do now?

Jasper sat at her feet and looked up expectantly. He meowed loudly. Suddenly she realized why he was there. "I forgot to feed you, didn't I?" Normally that was June's job. Now she had to pick up the slack on all the chores her partner shared with her.

Edda struggled to her feet and trudged to the kitchen. She didn't even try to feign interest in what Jasper got to eat, blindly reaching into the cupboard and pulling out the first can she found. She opened the tin and unceremoniously dumped the contents into Jasper's bowl. "There you go."

She leaned against the counter and watched the cat eat. Her last meal had been hours ago, but food was the last thing on her mind.

"For God's sake, woman, eat. You're all skin and bones." Edda swore she could hear June's words. It all seemed like too much trouble, but she settled for an apple to appease June's imagined disapproval. She sank her teeth into the fruit, all the while studying Jasper as he ate his food with gusto. The cat probably hadn't even realized June was gone.

Her next thought came five minutes later when she stared at an empty cat bowl and an apple core. She tossed the core into the bin and returned to the sofa. At that moment the bed held too many memories for her so she settled for the sofa in the living room. She pulled up a blanket and slid off into a fitful sleep.

†

Edda woke the next morning to the electronic shrill of her cell phone. She picked it up and looked at the displayed name. "Shit!" The ring persisted and reluctantly she answered. "Hello?"

"Where the hell were you yesterday? You left me in the lurch with *your* friends!"

"Hello Gail," Edda said flatly.

"It was your responsibility to be there!"

June's sister was a real pain in the ass but Edda bit her tongue. She so wanted to argue that she had been the one responsible for organizing June's funeral. All Gail had to do was be there. But she had no strength to fight.

"What do you want, Gail?"

"What do I want? I want an explanation!"

"I wasn't well."

"You should have stayed!"

"I didn't have time. Did you want me to vomit all over June's grave?" She wasn't sick really, but she knew Gail wouldn't accept anything less than death as an excuse.

"You should have sucked it up and stayed!"

"What is your problem?"

"My problem? She was your friend and you ran out on her!" Gail's voice rose in volume until she was yelling.

"She was my *partner*, Gail. I'm sure she would have understood."

"Well, you didn't know her very well."

"I…" Edda stopped herself from getting dragged into an argument. "Is there anything else?"

"Your friends will be contacting you. Just thought you should know." The phone went dead.

Edda lowered the cell from her ear. She looked at her hand and saw her fingers were white. "Shit! Shit! Shit!" She threw the phone on the sofa. "So it starts."

June had already settled her estate with Edda when she was alive in an effort to avoid the stress of a contest over her will. June had meticulously organized the transfer of her half of the apartment to Edda, even going so far as to get two independent psychiatric reports on the state of her mental health. June had no qualms about the ruthlessness of her sister who had always refused to accept her sexuality. Gail had always blamed Edda as the constant source of her wayward behavior.

†

Edda was right to be fearful. Over the next few weeks her cell constantly rang with friends and family asking about her welfare. She knew their concern was genuine but after the first thirty calls she had grown weary of answering the same questions. Edda had a fairly good idea who Gail had talked to and in what order. Those later down the list reported Gail's vitriol had become more animated. It galled Edda to have to apologize for Gail's complete lack of propriety on such a solemn occasion.

June certainly knew her family. Edda was tempted to not attend today's reading of the will at all because June had already shown it to her. Aside from the apartment, everything went to June's parents to disperse as they saw fit. They had discussed leaving the task to them because it was going to be messy. But Edda had to go to the reading if, for nothing else, than to support June's parents. They were a kind couple who had welcomed her into their family. Unlike Gail. Mike and Jenny had been interested in their daughter's life, but Gail lived in a world where only heterosexuals existed.

Edda braced herself for the ensuing battle as she sat on one of the chairs at the solicitor's office. She remained silent as the will was read, her gaze firmly set on Gail. Gail's jaw twitched as the words spilled from the solicitor's mouth. She was not happy.

"What about the apartment?" Gail turned her gaze on Edda.

"The apartment is not part of the will," Mr. Regis replied.

"What? She owns half of that!"

"June had already disposed of the property."

"Where's the money?"

"Her half of the property was signed over to Ms. Case."

"She doesn't deserve any part of the estate. After all, it wasn't as if she was married to my sister."

"There is more to this will that hasn't been read. Now, if I may… 'My share in an apartment at 81 Union Street goes to Ms. Edda Case. I have signed over this property to her before my death.'"

"That's not fair!"

"'This exchange has been duly notarized, and I have sought the opinion of two independent psychiatrists as to the state of my mind. This transaction is iron-clad, Gail, and cannot be contested.'" Mr. Regis looked up from the paper and stared at Gail, who snorted her disgust.

Mr. Regis looked at the paper once more. "'Should any part of this will be challenged, that person will no longer be a beneficiary.' I think that says it all."

Gail sat there fuming, while her husband, Graham, sat by her side squirming in his seat.

"My condolences to you all," Mr. Regis said. He rose from his seat and left the room to the family.

"How dare she—"

"Gail!" June's father stood and glared at her. "Shut up!" He moved the few steps to Edda and looked down. "Edda, I'm sorry for your loss. If you need anything, please don't hesitate to call."

Edda took the words as a chance to escape. She stood, nodded to June's mother and left without saying another word. Staying was not an option and she could hear Gail's voice even as she closed the door.

When she reached her apartment she poured herself a drink. Gail's ranting had been the final straw. She had to get out of the city. But where? She could just pack a bag and go. See where the road took her. But that went against her need for some organization in her life.

June had gotten a note from a mutual friend a while back about a respite at her house. Edda went to June's bedside table and opened the drawer. There was a mass of get well cards and letters stuffed into it and Edda was forced to empty the lot onto the bed. She sorted through the paper until she found what she was looking for.

Edda held the note in her hand and studied the words. When the invitation had first arrived, she had dismissed it. June was too ill to travel and she didn't want to be too far from the specialist. Now Edda needed to get away and the thought was appealing. Would the invitation still be open now that June had passed away? Edda reached for the phone.

"Hello?" Lesley's voice was bright and cheerful. It was not exactly what she wanted to hear but she couldn't begrudge the woman a life.

"Lesley? It's Edda."

"Edda? Oh God, Edda. How are you? When I heard the news…"

"Yeah, even when you know it's coming, it still kicks you in the gut."

"What do you need?" Lesley said even without the question.

"I was wondering if the offer of the house swap was still valid."

"Sure. In fact, it would help me a lot. My boss just opened up a new area office where you are and I have to go set it up. How long did you want?"

"I don't know. How long do you think your job will take?"

"It's probably a six-month project initially, but don't you worry about that. Take as long as you need. I can always find accommodation elsewhere."

Edda couldn't complain. Lesley was going out of her way to be accommodating. "Can we start with a couple of weeks?"

"Sure can. That will give me a bit of time to check out apartments for rent."

"You can always stay with me when I return."

No," Lesley said firmly, "you're not ready for that, but thanks for the offer."

"I'm a big girl, Lesley—"

"Edda, stop it! If you need to get away from your apartment then you're not going to cope with someone else living there."

Lesley was right. She wanted to escape from all the bereavement and constant phone calls. Having someone in the apartment with her was not a good idea. "When does your new post start?"

"Monday next week, but I can wait until you're ready —
"

"Next Monday's fine. Can I bring Jasper?" Not that she would go without him, but she asked anyway.

"Not a problem."

Edda knew Lesley was pandering to her request because Lesley didn't have pets. "Thanks, Lesley. You're a lifesaver."

"I hope not literally, hon."

Edda could hear the concern in Lesley's voice. "No! Good Lord, no! I just need some time by myself for a while. Don't worry, I'll be sniffing around work soon enough."

"What about work?"

"I can just as easily do it at your place as mine. It just means they have to travel a bit further to pick it up."

"They won't like that."

"If they don't like it, then tough shit!" Edda grumbled.

"That's my girl," Lesley said then chuckled.

After she had hung up Edda suddenly realized what she had agreed to. By next Monday she was leaving the apartment behind for a while. Everything that was June was in that apartment. Had her impulsive decision been right or wrong? Only time would tell.

Chapter Two

It was now Tuesday. Lesley had arrived the day before at Edda's apartment, as arranged, so Edda could fill her in on everything and hand over the keys.

Edda had used the few precious days beforehand to organize the disposal of June's things. No, not disposal. That was too harsh a word. Edda had lovingly touched everything that was June's as it passed through her hands on the way to a packing box. She wanted to make sure that all the memories stayed with her. To avoid any unnecessary needling from Gail, Edda had a courier pick up the boxes and only then contacted June's parents to tell them they were on their way. She asked them to tell everyone that she wanted her privacy respected, but they all knew who she was talking about. Edda wanted them to keep Gail on a leash.

Edda began to have second thoughts about going away. She'd felt sick packing June's clothes. She wasn't ready for such an upheaval, but Lesley was doing her a favor by allowing her to use her house for a while, and she certainly didn't want to subject the woman to Gail.

Before she left the city Edda bought herself a disposable cell. She wanted to make sure she got her privacy, and taking her own cell wouldn't give her that. She contacted her mother, her agent, Tamara, and Lesley and gave them each the number with strict instructions not to give it out to anybody, especially Gail. If she needed to be contacted in a hurry then they could do so themselves.

It was a strange feeling to toss her cell into a drawer and leave it there. It had been her lifeline for so long it was foreign not to have it with her, but she knew if she had it she might as well stay put in her own apartment.

Edda arrived at Lesley's house late in the afternoon on Tuesday. Her GPS had been a real pain in the ass, sending her the wrong way up a one-way street and nearly depositing her in a lake before finally getting her to the right destination. How could the GPS companies justify their price tag when they couldn't even navigate properly? The feminine voice had been soothing at first, but after the two near-misses she was on edge whenever a voice calmly said "turn right."

The first thing Edda took out of the car was the kitty litter tray. She carried it into the kitchen and filled it. If Jasper felt anything like she did, he'd need to use it straightaway. Edda pulled out the cat box and carried Jasper through to the kitchen. She placed the carrier on the table and pulled him out. He meowed pitifully before giving her a scowl. "Yeah, I know. It was a long trip." She put him down next to the tray. He sniffed at it for a moment before treading carefully into the middle of it. He looked up at her. "You're shy all of a sudden? Fine." Edda was too tired to argue. If the cat would do his business quicker she'd turn away. She heard the crinkle of litter as Jasper walked over it. "How about some dinner?" Jasper looked up at her and meowed again. He brushed his head along her leg as he prowled around her. "I have to get it out of the car, you crazy cat."

There was no time to argue with a cat on the verge of starvation, she decided. Edda went out to the car, grabbed the box of groceries and dug around for his cat bowl. Until Jasper was settled everything else would have to wait.

The cat sat expectantly next to the bowl while Edda wrestled with the ring on the can. He cried piteously. "I'm hurrying." The tin finally popped and the lid tore away slowly. Edda aimed the tin at the bowl and flicked hard. The food slopped and nearly hit Jasper on the head in his hurry to reach the food. "Idiot." Jasper ignored her from that point on as he dug into his dinner.

Edda had no such urge, but she could certainly use a coffee. She scanned the kitchen, taking in the position of the various implements and utensils. The setup was similar to her own and she felt she would have little trouble settling in. Edda reached for the coffeemaker and filled it with water. Once it started to make some noise, Edda left Jasper to quickly unpack her car. When Jasper finished his meal his attention would be elsewhere and she would be close behind him to keep him out of trouble. If she wanted any hope of having something to sleep in she had to take her opportunity now.

She thought she was going to make it but on her second to the last load, Jasper met her in the hall. "Don't you have something to do?" He sat at her feet and looked up. She knew that look. He was ready for some cuddling. Considering the long trip, she couldn't blame him.

With some resignation she opened the front door a crack and aimed her electronic key at the car. When the car beeped at her she closed the door. Any chance of collecting the one remaining load would have to wait. "Come on, you lazy thing." She walked into the kitchen, made her coffee and retired to the living room. She snatched up the remote and made herself comfortable on the sofa. Even before she had switched on the TV the cat had jumped up and was sniffing around her. He crawled onto her lap and dropped. "Where's the 'please,' huh?" Not that she expected Jasper to ever ask. No, he was one of those cats who would act first then ask.

Edda paid scant attention to the television and idly stroked Jasper's fur. It had been a long, long day and she was ready to sleep. The monotonous drone of the TV anchor's voice was mesmerizing. Before she knew it, her eyes closed.

†

The sound of the news assaulted Edda's ears. Had she only just nodded off? Jasper sat on her chest and licked his paw. "Meeoowww."

"What time is it?" She looked around in confusion. Light filtered through the lace curtain. "It's morning?" Edda checked the time in the bottom corner of the television. "Six thirty?" She gave Jasper a glance. Had he behaved? Did she really want to find out? "How much trouble did you get into?"

"Meeoowww."

Edda thought it sounded like a guilty admission but she'd only find out if she moved. Jasper settled down where he was, curling his tail around his prone body. "Comfortable?" she asked. Jasper purred loudly. As it was obvious she wasn't moving any time soon, Edda closed her eyes. A few moments later, her eyes popped open. "No." She swiped Jasper away and watched as he moved to the end of the sofa and curled up. "I'm not going to let you be in charge." But they both knew that wasn't going to happen. Since June's death, Jasper had ruled the roost, being Edda's lifeline to her current existence.

She swung her legs off the sofa and onto the floor. It took a lot of energy to pull herself up into the seated position and she sat there while her heart rate dropped to its normal beat. Edda glanced at the cat, who had already forgotten her presence and had closed his eyes. The sofa, her back told her, was not a good place to sleep, and at some point during the day she would have to work the kinks out of her body.

While Jasper was asleep Edda finished unpacking the car. Finding homes for her things was not what she really wanted to do, but it was a necessity. The chore proved invaluable. While putting things away she discovered where Lesley kept her things, and she put to memory many items that would come in handy later.

Later. How long did she expect to be here? She had only agreed to two weeks, so memorizing everything would be a waste of her time. Would two weeks be enough? Would it be too much? It was a matter of asking herself that question at the end of the allotted time. When she was finally satisfied with the arrangement of her things Edda grabbed a coffee and a book then went outside to the backyard to survey her neighborhood for the next two weeks.

It was pleasant enough. The home was on the edge of a new estate built ten years ago. Her backyard had a panoramic view of a large field and in the middle of the field sat a few trees nestled on the top of a short rise, looking very much like a tiny island in the middle of a very large sea.

She sipped her coffee as she stared across the abandoned expanse of land, her mind not thinking of anything in particular. It was nice to be away from the constant chatter, at least for a while.

Edda turned her attention back to the house and studied the small backyard. She claimed the outdoor lounge and stretched herself out. The sun was out and warming her skin nicely. Would a few minutes do any harm? Any longer, she knew, would court disaster as far as Jasper was concerned. Past experience had taught her that a bored Jasper was a dangerous thing. Back at her apartment she possessed a sofa that had torn fabric from one of his moments of boredom, along with shredded curtains and a scratched bureau. But she would risk it. She put down her mug and opened the book, losing herself in someone else's life for a while.

"Hi there!"

Edda looked up from her book to see the ruggedly handsome face of the neighbor next door.

"Should I be calling the police?" he asked.

Edda remained silent and stared at him.

"I'm David Elliott, and you are…" he trailed off in the hope of getting an answer.

"Edda," she said warily.

"Edda. And what's a beautiful woman like you lounging around a home that I know you don't own?"

"David, was it?"

"Yes."

"One moment." Edda put down her book and stood up from the lounge. She had remembered an envelope sitting on the dining table when she arrived, and the name David rang a bell. As she expected, the envelope was still sitting on the table. Edda grabbed it and wandered back outside. She handed it over the fence, noting David's fingers brushing her hand.

"Thank you, Edda," he said silkily.

"No problem." She returned to the lounge and sat down, stretching herself out on the length of the seat. Edda could hear the rustle of paper as David opened the envelope and removed its contents. She closed her eyes and hoped that he would leave her alone.

"I see. You are house-sitting for a while."

"It's more a house-exchange program. She's living in my apartment." She immediately regretted saying it because now he would think it was an invitation to have a conversation.

"And what brings you here to our little community?"

"Change of scenery."

"Well then, how about…"

"David, please, I'm not interested in socializing right now."

"All right, I'll contact you…"

"No, thank you."

"But—"

"I just want to be left alone."

"Sorry, I…I…" He backed away. "I'll see you around then."

"Thank you, David. I'll talk to you later." *Damn*, she thought. Now he would think she was a bitch of the first order. Suddenly, she felt guilty for wanting to be alone, but he was pushing for information and a date and she didn't want to fight against giving either.

David backed away from the fence, but Edda could feel his presence on the other side. Was he going to try to instigate another conversation? Just in case, she picked up her book and retired inside.

Edda stood at the kitchen sink and looked out the window to the backyard. Lesley had warned her about David, but she thought she would have more time before she had to face him. Obviously, he got home early from his trip. She had been there only a day and already she was faced with, according to Lesley, the nosiest neighbor in the United States, possibly the world.

David was the last person she needed right now, not as a neighbor or a date, and certainly not as a friend. She was just getting her head around June's death and making a step or two toward wanting to get out of bed in the morning. The last thing she needed right now was a cheerful man trying to make a date with her.

"Brrrowww."

Edda felt the gentle wisp of hair brush her leg. She leaned down and picked up the cat. "What do you think, Jasper? Should I move now before he has a chance to make me a friend?" Jasper answered with a pitiful cry. "Or should I ignore all this and just feed you?" Jasper purred loudly. "Food it is."

She put Jasper down and found the tin of cat food on the first try. She sighed heavily. And she had just packed her things away…

Chapter Three

Edda woke in the middle of the night to the sound of a clattering garbage bin. She looked at the illuminated alarm clock. Two o'clock. Dragged from her drug-laden sleep she thought it was Jasper, but a gentle nudge from the feline told her he was snuggled up against her leg. Edda fought the sleeping pill to try and listen for another sound. As the drug slowly pulled her back to sleep the night remained silent.

Her next thought was inspired by the shrill squeal of the bedside alarm. *Was it seven already?* It seemed only moments ago her head had hit the pillow and her last thought was of June. Something had happened during the night but she couldn't remember what it was. Involuntarily, her gaze swept over the covers and settled on Jasper. Was it something to do with the cat? She wasn't sure, but obviously it wasn't important otherwise she would have remembered it.

Reluctantly she threw back the covers and swung her legs over the side of the bed. Edda sat there and stared at the floor. Today's timetable was pretty much the same as it had been all week. Maybe it was time for a change.

Jasper stirred and stretched. He rolled onto his back and playfully batted Edda's arm. She reached out and stroked his stomach, eliciting a loud purr and a soft meow. Whenever she stopped stroking, Jasper swatted her. He wasn't ready for her to stop any time soon.

"What do you say, Jasper? Is it time for breakfast?"

The cat stopped hitting her and stared as if he understood what she said. He rolled over to his side and lay there expectantly.

"One of us has to make the first move. I suppose it's going to be me." It took a lot of energy to sit up and she was nearly tempted to forego the early rise and sleep in. After all, she had nowhere particular to go and no appointments, so her time was her own. If she wanted to sleep in that was her choice.

Edda decided it was time to give herself a stern talking to. "Come on, you old bag, get up." Jasper rolled onto his feet and strolled the few inches over to her side. He stroked himself against her arm time and again, rubbing from his head to the tip of his tail before turning and repeating his movement, as she considered her options. "You know if you go back to bed that's just the beginning." She knew whiling away her time in bed would be the beginning of a bad habit, and maybe the start of something more serious—her withdrawal from life.

With some effort she hauled herself to her feet. Jasper protested at her sudden movement, nearly falling off the bed when she removed her arm. Edda grabbed the cat and headed for the kitchen. She padded downstairs in bare feet and regretted it when her feet touched the tile floor.

"Why didn't you say something?" She glared at the cat and then at the mess he'd obviously made overnight.

"Bbrroowww," Jasper purred.

"Yeah, you don't fool me, you overgrown garbage disposal." Edda put him down and placed a handful of dry cat food in the bowl. He looked up at her expectantly. "Sorry, cat, that's it for this morning." Jasper sniffed at the bowl and walked away. "You'll come crawling back. You always do."

Edda cleaned up Jasper's mess then reached for the coffeemaker and pressed the button. She couldn't do another thing until she had her first coffee fix for the day. While she waited, Edda looked out the window. The sun was disgustingly bright and the birds were chirping too cheerfully. She wasn't ready for so much happiness.

The liquid began to drip into the cup and the air filled with the scent of brewing coffee. Edda fetched the milk from the refrigerator and stood in front of the coffeemaker, willing it to finish dripping. She snatched away the cup as the last drops fell and she topped up the cup with milk. She ignored the heat and took a sip. The scalding coffee hit her stomach like a bomb, but she didn't care. The sudden pain woke her up.

She stepped outside and took a deep breath. Her first opinion of the day was correct; it was too cheerful for her state of mind. The coffee cup went to her lips automatically, and before she knew it the cup was empty. She contemplated a second cup but decided against it. There was still the rest of the day ahead of her, so it would be wise to pace her coffee addiction.

Just as she was about to return inside, she noticed the fallen garbage can. The lid lay beside it and half the contents scattered around the can. She put down her cup and picked up the rubbish, replacing the lid with a bang. Suddenly last night's awakening came to mind. "Damn cats."

Edda returned to the kitchen and washed her cup. Breakfast didn't seem appealing, so she decided on a walk instead. Maybe the exercise would stimulate her appetite.

Ten minutes later she stepped out the front door, slipping on her sunglasses before stepping down the path to the sidewalk. One way looked as appealing as the other. Turning to her right would force her to walk past David's house and that was enough to make her turn left.

The neighborhood was surprisingly noisy. Birds were cheeping, a dog barked, and a passing car beeped, its occupants waving at her. It was then that she had an epiphany. Despite her grief, life went on around her. She hadn't thought of it that way before. While her world had stopped, the rest of humanity carried on with everyday life.

"Well, hello there."

Edda drew her attention away from her thoughts to see who was talking to her. *Oh no.* "Hello, David," she said flatly. She should have turned right in the first place. "What are you doing here?"

"I live here. What's your excuse?" He smiled brightly at her.

"Exercise."

"Ah." He watched her and she felt herself squirm.

"Well, I better keep going—"

"Do you want some company?" He interrupted her before she could make her escape.

"Look, David—"

"Let me show you the neighborhood," he prompted, turning around to fall in beside her.

How could she say no without coming off as sounding like a snooty bitch? She couldn't. "Great." Edda started to walk and David kept up easily with her pace.

"So what brings you to our little community?"

"Change of scenery."

"So you said yesterday."

"Then why ask me again?" Edda winced after the words came out.

"Look." David stopped in his tracks. "Obviously, something's happened that's made you distant. Let me help you."

Edda pulled up. "Maybe I don't want help. Did you ever think of that?"

"What happened?" he said softly.

Edda made the mistake of looking into his eyes. There was no condescension or malice, only concern. "I'm not looking for any new entanglements. I just lost my partner a month ago." The words tumbled from her mouth unheeded. She hadn't meant to reveal so much.

"I'm so sorry." He touched her arm and she flinched. "I mean it, Edda. It must be very hard for you."

"You have no idea."

"How long were you with him?"

She picked up on the word "him." Should she correct him? How would he take the news? "We were together twelve years." She decided on a noncommittal answer.

"That's a long time. And he never proposed to you?"

"We decided the arrangement was all we could have." Not that they had any choice about it.

"That's pretty sad. He couldn't even give you a commitment after twelve years?"

"The cancer cut it short. I really don't want to talk about it right now."

"Sad memories. I understand."

They continued their walk, making their way up one street and down another. While this was the outskirts of suburbia, the neighborhood seemed almost like a dream. The only thing missing from the scene were the white picket fences.

Finally they had come full circle and passed David's house. "Would you like to come in for a coffee?"

"Don't you have to work?"

"I have a few days off. I've been overseas on work and they owe me."

"David, as I said before I'm not interested—"

"How about as a friend? You can do that, can't you?"

She had to admit the man was persistent. "Please—"

"Come on. I won't jump you or anything." He grinned at her.

He was giving her no choice but to deliver the news. "I'm old enough to be your mother."

"Oh, tosh! You can't be more than forty."

"Thank you." She had to smile at his obvious compliment. "Add another ten or so years and you're in the ballpark."

"So? Age never really scared me."

Edda sighed. She braced herself for the reaction to the next statement. "Does being a lesbian scare you?"

"I never really thought of myself as a lesbian," he quipped.

"I'm being serious here."

"So am I. Come on in for a coffee." He was serious.

Unless she was blatantly rude, Edda had run out of excuses. Come hell or high water, David was determined to be her friend. He extended his hand to her and waited for her to take it.

The next thing she knew she was standing on his doorstep. Apparently her feet had made the decision before her mind had a chance to think about it.

"Come on in." He stood aside to allow her to precede him.

To her surprise the home was neat and tidy. If she didn't know that he was a raging heterosexual she would wonder if he was gay. "Nice place," she said politely.

"Thanks. Come on through." He led the way past the living room to the kitchen. "It's cozier in here." He extended his hand toward an empty chair. After she was seated he moved to the kettle. "How do you take it?"

"Cream."

"No sugar?"

"Nope. Straight up."

He chuckled. "Cup or mug?"

"Mug is fine, thanks."

"A woman after my own heart."

"David—"

"Sorry. I forgot." He put the coffee in the mugs and sat down opposite her while the water boiled. "Why are all the beautiful ones gay?"

"Because we've figured you out?"

David laughed loudly. "Ahh. That's a good sign."

"That we've figured you out? I thought it would have the opposite effect."

"No, hearing you make a joke. You need to laugh more."

"I haven't felt like laughing much lately."

His hand moved to rest on top of Edda's. "I'm truly sorry. It must have been devastating."

Edda stared out his kitchen window. "You think you're ready for it, but when it comes it just rips your heart out." She could feel the tears welling up.

"How long did you know?"

"Six months. She hadn't been feeling well for a year before that but they couldn't find the cause."

"They had a year to find cancer?" He sounded stunned.

"Nothing showed up for a long time. By the time it announced its arrival it was too late. That's just the way it is. Sometimes you get lucky and find it early enough. Other times…well, June wasn't that lucky."

The kettle whistled and David stood to make the coffee. They were silent until he sat down again, mugs in hand.

"We'd been offered to stay at Lesley's house before June passed away, you know."

"But you didn't take it."

"No, June was too sick to travel and she wanted to be near her specialist. I think it was more for my benefit so I didn't get caught with an emergency I couldn't handle."

"That's understandable. Still, you would've missed me if you had." Edda said nothing. "Aha! That thrilled to meet me, huh?"

She just smiled. She couldn't tell him that Lesley thought he was nosy. Edda thought he was lonely. Time would tell.

"I just wasn't up to being happy, David."

"I see that now, but I think you need someone to talk to; someone who's a stranger." He looked at her pleadingly.

"Why, David? Why get burdened with my problems?"

"Because you need a shoulder to cry on…and because I like you. Are you sure you're gay?"

"Positive." However, he was right about someone to talk to. Hadn't she only thought about crawling into bed and never getting out an hour ago? "But I may take you up on the spare shoulder."

"Yeah?"

"Yeah." Was she going to regret this?

"Then let me make you some breakfast. You're all skin and bones."

"I thought you said I was fine."

"I lied." He grinned broadly at her before reaching for a skillet.

"Just toast."

"That's not a healthy breakfast."

"And that skillet you're waving around is not healthy either."

"This?" He put the pan down on the stove with a flourish. "Only if you have a low-iron diet."

Edda rolled her eyes. The guy thought he was a comedian.

"Too corny? How about some scrambled eggs then? I'll throw in the toast for free."

"I hope you don't make a living with those jokes."

"I wish." He found a bowl and carried some eggs from the refrigerator.

Edda stood up from the kitchen table and took a seat at the bench. "A chef then?"

"Nope. I only cook for survival, I'm afraid." Still, he broke the eggs with a quick rap and one-handed. For a hack cook he was remarkably adept. "And you?" He asked the question without looking at her. His attention was on the mixture in the bowl.

"Same as you. I work long hours so the last thing I want to do when I get home is to cook."

"Ahh, you cheat."

"I'm afraid so. I don't have the time or the inclination to be creative."

"Dare I ask what you do for a living?"

Edda hesitated. Did she want to reveal too much to someone who was a stranger to her? "Let's start with you."

"I've got nothing to hide. I'm middle management."

"That covers a wide area. Middle management of what?"

"Life insurance."

"I can see why you didn't want to say." He laughed. "Has anyone taken any potshots at you lately?"

"Only verbally, but I don't do sales anymore. I do the occasional visit to the state offices to rally the troops, except for this last trip. All the rest is just plain old paperwork."

Edda studied David. "You don't look like an insurance salesman."

"It's all part of the disguise." He gently stirred the eggs until they were cooked. "Personally, I thought I sucked at selling insurance. Maybe it's my personality. Still, I rose to my level of incompetence in middle management. At least it got me out of hounding people for money."

"I'd have to agree with you."

"That I found my level of incompetence?"

"No, that your sunny disposition doesn't go with life insurance. Why did you stay?"

He stopped for a moment and thought. "Laziness, I suppose. Pay was good. I got to travel. The promotion got me out of sales. I couldn't be bothered to start from scratch in another profession."

"That's brutally honest."

He shrugged his shoulders before he plated up two servings of scrambled eggs and toast.

Edda felt her hunger stir. "It looks pretty good."

"Pretty good? I should be insulted." David took the two plates to the kitchen table and set them down. "There you go, madam." He fumbled around in a drawer for knives and forks.

Edda moved to the table and sat down. The food did look appealing and it was the first time she actually felt like eating. She waited for David to sit down and start before she tucked in. "Not bad."

"All these compliments might go to my head."

Edda smiled then continued to delve into David's insurance career while they ate. Soon Edda looked down and was surprised to realize she had eaten everything on her plate.

"More?" David asked politely.

"No thanks. That's more than I've eaten in quite a while."

David finished his eggs then stood and grabbed her mug, not even asking if she wanted a refill.

"So Miss Edda."

"Case. Edda Case."

"Well, Case, Edda Case, what do you do for a living?"

"A bit of this and that."

"That covers a wide area. A bit of this and that what?"

"Touché," Edda replied. He had turned the verbal tables back on her. "I sell ladies' handbags."

"Uh-huh." David stared at her dubiously.

"I do."

"Sure. You can afford to take six months off work. There's more to it than that."

"Are you sure you're not a detective?"

"Nope. Not in this life or any other." He leaned against the countertop. "Now spill it."

"All right. I design ladies handbags."

"Have I heard of you?"

"Probably not. My work is more custom-made rather than mass market."

"So, exclusive huh?"

"You could say that."

"How much would a bag of yours cost?"

Edda didn't like talking shop with a stranger. "Let's just say, depending on what you want, it could be anything from four to five figures."

"Ahh. So you can afford a six-month holiday."

"Who said anything about it being a holiday?"

David's eyebrow rose. "Okay, it's six months of mourning." Edda's lips turned down. "I'm sorry, honey. I didn't mean to upset you." He came over to where she was seated and crouched down next to her, holding her hand gently. "Things will be all right. You'll see."

"But I don't want them to be all right. They'll never be all right again." Edda felt the tear slide down her cheek, tickling her facial hairs as it went. "I don't want to go on without her."

"You need something to keep you busy."

"I need June."

"Edda, you can't have June. I can do many things, but that's not one of them." His hand came up and brushed away the tear. "It's not going to mean much right at the moment, but given time things will get better."

"And what do I do in the meantime? It's eating me up inside."

"You need to keep yourself occupied."

"With what? I don't have any hobbies. Work was my hobby."

"I've still got a few days coming to me. How about we explore the neighborhood together?"

Edda could see he was serious. "Why, David? You know you don't have a chance with me. Why waste your time?"

"It's not about sex, my dear Edda. You need a friend right now and I'm available." He looked sheepishly at her. "Actually, Lesley had already brought me up to speed before she left and asked me to keep an eye on you. She figured you would need company."

"Why that…"

"Now hold it. Lesley was worried. She thought you could use a helping hand."

"I wasn't going to kill myself, if that's what she was thinking." Edda felt a sense of betrayal.

"No, she wasn't thinking that," he said carefully, "but she knew moving into a new neighborhood, alone, would be stressful. On top of that you have grief and possibly depression to contend with, and it's a recipe for..."

"Disaster?"

"Let's just say heartache. I'm here to ease the way."

"I left my apartment to get away from this kind of meddling." Edda saw David's body stiffen. *Oh crap.* "I'm sorry, David, I didn't mean—"

"More coffee?" David asked, even though both of them knew he had just refilled the cups.

"Sit down," she said.

Grumpily he complied, even though his severely dented ego fought it.

"Look at me." When his gaze refused to meet hers she barked, "David!"

"You've made your point."

"Rather clumsily, I'm afraid." She tried a smile. "I'm really tired and my brain is mush. I wasn't prepared for your happy face to greet me as soon as I arrived. Do you understand?" It didn't garner a response. "How can I make it right?" It was the perfect opportunity to get rid of David and his chirpy disposition once and for all and here she was trying to make amends. Was she crazy?

"It's okay," he said quietly.

She was about to let the matter rest when a little voice whispered inside her head to speak. "No, it's not all right. It was a horrible thing to say and was totally uncalled for. It was a knee-jerk reaction. I'm sorry."

David's body relaxed and he looked at her. "Thanks."

She reached across the table and patted his hand. "Are you sure you're not gay?"

"Oh, believe me, I am certainly straight."

"And you're still not married?" Edda was glad for the change of subject. Apparently David was too.

"Hey! It's not from lack of trying. I'm still waiting for Miss Right." He looked her in the eye. "Maybe you can find Miss Right for me. That'd be a good hobby."

"Oh no." Edda held up her hand. "No, no, no, no. I'm no matchmaker. Besides, I'm not in the right frame of mind at the moment. I'll settle for the walks." David grinned triumphantly and Edda sputtered, "You…you…weasel. That's what you wanted all along."

"You can thank me later."

"I'm not thanking you now. What makes you think I'll thank you later?"

"Just a hunch."

After eliciting a promise to leave her alone for the rest of the day, Edda agreed to an early morning hike around the neighborhood the next day.

✝

She wasn't sure whether it was the eggs David served her at breakfast or the can of soup she found in the cupboard for dinner, but something disagreed with her. On her third visit to the bathroom that night, Edda decided that she needed to check the use by date on the can. This time she didn't bother switching on the light and just threw up into the bowl she knew was there. Her stomach cramped and her sides ached from the heaving, but there was nothing she could do about it.

She really missed June. Whenever she'd been sick, June's comforting presence was usually enough to make her feel better. Now she didn't even have that. It was lonely without her, and being sick made her forlorn and miserable.

31

When the retching finally subsided Edda moved to the sink. Blindly her hand slapped around for the washcloth. She put it under the cold water and applied the cool towel to her face, wiping away all evidence of her sickness. As she rinsed out the cloth, her gaze wandered out the window.

From that particular window Edda had a clear view to the copse of trees in the middle of the field behind the property. A bright yellow ball of light glowed at the edge of the woods. She squinted in an effort to focus on the nocturnal activity. As hard as she tried, she couldn't make out what was going on. "Damn it!"

Edda put on her slippers and plodded down the staircase, through the house and out into the backyard. A few steps onto the grass and something hit her in the face. She staggered back and felt a wetness coming from her nose. Unwittingly, she stepped forward and was hit again. The last thing she remembered was the pain and the darkness.

Chapter Four

Edda came to but immediately knew it wasn't where she had passed out. It was indoors for one, and it smelled like a hospital. She opened her eyes but found that her vision was impeded. Something sat heavily across her nose and, reaching up, she tried to remove it.

"Don't do that."

"David?" she croaked. "What happened?"

"You knocked yourself out."

"I did? How?"

"There was a shovel on the lawn. You must have stepped on it."

She didn't remember leaving a shovel on the lawn. In fact, she hadn't touched a garden implement since her arrival.

"What…what's this?" Her hand touched the gauze.

"You broke your nose. They had to operate."

"There go the looks."

"Give it a couple of weeks and you'll be back to your beautiful self."

"David…"

"Oh, come on Edda. You're a beautiful woman."

She conceded that David had ignored the fact that her nose was crooked and her eyes were too wide apart. "Well, the nose might be straight now."

"That's my girl," he said.

Edda cleared her throat.

"Woman?"

Edda glared at him.

"Friend?"

The silence was deafening.

"Acquaintance? Oh, you know what I mean."

There was a hint of movement in Edda's peripheral vision. It was a nurse.

"Ahh, she's awake. How are you feeling Ms. Case?"

She didn't know how to answer that one. An idiot? Sore? Tired? All of the above? Edda settled for the most obvious one. "Fine."

As she spoke, the nurse shoved a digital thermometer into her mouth. Her hand found Edda's wrist and her fingertips sat over her pulse point.

Edda glanced at David who had wandered over to the window while the nurse took her readings. She looked at the woman studying her watch. What did it take to be a nurse? Edda didn't think she could stand being around sick people all day, let alone be happy about it.

The nurse pulled out the thermometer and glanced at it. She smiled at Edda and moved around to the end of the bed to record her stats on the chart. "Another ten minutes, Ms. Case."

"For what?"

"Visitors." She looked at David standing at the window.

"Thank you, errr…" Edda finished awkwardly.

"Delia. I'll be by later to help you clean up."

"Clean…up." Edda's brow furrowed unsuccessfully. The padding and plaster across her face pulled and it stung with the effort. "Oh. Fine. Thank you." She waited until the nurse left. "You've been shown the door."

"It sounds like it."

"What's the real damage?"

"I don't know. Since I'm not a relative, they won't tell me." He moved toward her bed and frowned at her. "You really know how to avoid a morning walk, don't you?"

"I'll take a rain check."

"You bet your booties, you will." He smiled and reached for her hand. "I'm sorry you got hurt. Do you remember what happened?" He sat on the edge of her bed.

"I wasn't feeling well. It was about one o'clock and I looked out the bathroom window. There was a light shining in the trees in the field behind my house."

"Are you sure?"

"I wasn't imagining it, David. That was the reason I went outside. So I could get a better look over the fence."

"Then you knocked yourself out."

"I don't remember a shovel on the back lawn. I haven't done any gardening since I've been here."

"Well, someone put it there."

"Why? What's the point?"

"They wanted to surprise you with a clean garden?"

"This is serious."

"I agree. It's serious enough for you to break your nose."

"Don't remind me."

"We can go and check the woods when you're discharged, okay?"

"What about work?"

"I've still got the rest of the week. If you want I can take some holidays."

"I'm quite capable of looking after myself." David's lips tightened. "Except for the shovel thing." All the while she had been talking the plaster over her nose had gradually shifted and was now pressing on her swollen flesh. Her hand rose and gently pushed the plaster to relieve the pressure.

"Don't do that." Edda could hear the concern in David's voice.

"It was pushing against a bruise."

"Oh."

There was the sound of a bell and David looked silently at her. "It looks like my time is up."

"Thank you for the visit."

"My pleasure. I just wish I wasn't visiting you in a hospital." David leaned in and brushed his lips over Edda's forehead. "Be a good girl and do what the nurses tell you."

"Yes, *brother*." She said "brother" emphatically to warn him. The kiss was completely wasted on her, and she wanted him to stop trying to convert her. He grinned at her then turned around and left.

Edda didn't know what to make of her neighbor. He was either trying to woo her into changing teams or he was gay. Whichever one it was, he was ingratiating himself into her life very quickly and she wasn't sure she liked it.

†

Edda must have dozed off because the next thing she was aware of was Delia standing by her bed. Her head jerked up and she immediately regretted it.

"Easy there." Delia's hand rested on Edda's arm. Her hand swiftly moved to her wrist and grasped it to take her pulse. Edda watched the nurse, whose attention was on the watch attached to her uniform. "Ahh, there it is. Your pulse was racing there for a minute."

"No wonder. You scared me to death."

"Not quite." Delia looked up at her. "You've still got a pulse."

Despite herself, Edda chuckled. She hadn't had much to laugh about recently. David was doing his best to keep up a steady stream of one-liners, which amused her, but the nurse's comment caught her off guard.

"How long will I be here?" She wanted the important information first.

"A few days. You were unconscious so the doctor wants to keep you in for observation."

"And the nose?"

"The cast should be gone before you leave. The doctor will have the final word on that."

"Do you know who brought me in?"

"I'm sorry, no. You may have to check with the EMTs."

"When was I admitted?"

"I've only been on ward for a few hours, but..." Delia went to the end of the bed and lifted the chart. "It says you were admitted at...four a.m. yesterday."

"Yesterday!" Edda grabbed her head as the word reverberated through it. "Yesterday?" she whispered. *Where did yesterday go?*

Delia scanned the notes attached to the clipboard. "Surgery was performed later in the morning. You woke up once but dozed off quickly."

"I don't remember that."

"I'll make a note of that." Delia grabbed the pen from her breast pocket and wrote on the paper.

Edda winced. She should have kept her mouth shut because she knew that piece of information would cost her another day or two in bed, and probably an X-ray or three.

Delia disappeared and Edda thought she had finally been left alone. A minute later Delia returned with a basin and towel.

"Oh, no." Edda held up her hands. "No, no, no."

"Don't be silly. You don't have anything I haven't seen before."

"Couldn't I just have a shower?"

"You've had a serious knock to the head. Besides, we have to keep the wound dry. Don't worry, you'll be up soon enough. But now…" Delia grabbed the curtain and pulled it around Edda's bed. "… there's time for a quick sponge bath."

"Now?" Edda pulled the sheet up tightly around her neck. "I'm fine…really."

Delia lathered up the washcloth and held it ready. "Don't be silly. This will make you feel better."

"No, it won't." Edda could see the determined gleam in her eye and reluctantly dropped the sheet. When Delia moved in, she closed her eyes and tried to think of anything else but the woman sponging her down. "You may want to get your husband to bring a nightgown and toiletries next time he's here."

"He's not my husband," Edda murmured.

"All right, your boyfriend then."

"He's not…never mind." What was the point in arguing? Edda had a sudden thought and sat upright.

"What?" Delia stopped scrubbing. "What's wrong?"

"My cat! The poor thing's in the house alone."

"Oh, your non-boyfriend said something about the cat. I think he's looking after it."

Edda settled back down and Delia continued to rub. "Roll on to your side." Edda reluctantly did so and jumped when the washcloth hit her ass.

"How embarrassing." Edda imagined her blush was making its way across her backside as she spoke.

"Oh, I don't know." The washing stopped. "As asses go, it's pretty good."

Edda smiled again and regretted it as the plaster pulled taut across her nose. "Don't make me laugh."

The cloth continued downward past her ass, wiping along her thighs and down to her toes. Delia paid attention to each toe and crevice, wiping away any dried sweat that had accumulated there. When the washcloth started its upward journey to her thighs, Edda's hands intervened. "I, errr…"

Delia chuckled. She washed out the cloth and handed it over to her patient. "You can do it yourself." She disappeared while Edda wiped between her legs, reappearing moments later with new bedsheets. She rinsed out the cloth and lathered it up again, handing it over to Edda to complete her wash. Delia stripped back the sheet and blanket while Edda washed her stomach and breasts, studiously concentrating on the bedcovers while she did so.

Delia handed over a fresh hospital gown, smiling as Edda struggled into it. "Here, let me." Edda reluctantly presented her back for the ties to be closed. "You can sit here while I change the bed."

Strong arms encircled Edda's waist and guided her to the visitor's seat next to her bed. She felt a little unsteady on her feet and realized that a shower was probably beyond her physical ability for now. Edda watched Delia change the bed quickly and efficiently. "Can I get you to change my bed at home?" she muttered.

"Sure. Are you having problems?"

It took a moment for Edda to realize she was kidding. "It takes me forever to make the bed. I can't get the damned hospital corners right."

"Practice. It takes lots and lots of practice." Delia finished making the bed and cleared away the basin. She returned for the soiled sheets.

Edda looked out the window. The weather had deteriorated somewhat so being where she was had one thing in its favor. However, all the minus points to her location far outweighed the fact that she wasn't out in the rain.

"Do you want to sit for a while or get back into bed?"

Edda shrugged. She had nothing to do.

Delia walked to the side of the bed. "There's TV. Here's the remote." Edda shook her head and turned her attention to the window. A moment later she returned her gaze to the bed but Delia was gone.

She stared out the window, watching the rivulets of water run down the panes of glass. If June was around…Edda stopped thinking. June. She had managed to put aside her sorrow for a while, but now it returned with a vengeance. Her tears stung her eyes but she couldn't stop them.

"Hey." Delia had returned and talked to her softly. "We're not supposed to get the incision wet." She circled the bed and reached for a tissue. "Come on." She returned to Edda's side and gently mopped up the tears.

"I'm sorry. It just hit me."

"Your nose will look good as new."

"No, it's not that."

"Did you lose a loved one?"

"Yes, I did. About two months ago. I was just thinking if…" Edda stopped short of saying "she," "I wouldn't be here if my partner was still alive."

"How did he die?"

"Cancer." Edda was not going to correct her.

"Nasty disease," Delia said. She pointed to the bed. "Do you want to return to bed?"

Edda wondered if she could get any sleep, but sitting where she was did nothing to cheer her up. "I think so."

Delia lifted up a handful of magazines. "I found these. They're a little out of date—"

"Thank you." Edda waited for Delia to lay the magazines to the bedside table.

"Here's an apple juice. Dinner will be in an hour. Get some rest."

Edda felt Delia's arm around her waist and welcomed the support. "Thank you for everything."

"You're most welcome. Ring if you need anything. The doctor will be around to see you after dinner."

Edda watched Delia leave and found herself alone. It was cold in that room, more from the realization that she had no one close she could call on for support. The only people she knew were David, whom she had met two days ago, and the nurse who had brought her some apple juice.

"Ahem, are you Edda Case?" Two EMTs stood at the door.

"Yes, I am."

"Your nurse said you were after some information."

"I was wondering how I got here?"

"In our vehicle."

Edda smiled wryly. Everyone was a comedian. "Who called it in?"

"We were met at the scene by a man who introduced himself as your neighbor."

"David?"

"Yes, I think that was the name he used."

How did David know of her accident?

"What time was that?"

"Around two thirty in the morning. He showed us through to your backyard. You shouldn't leave things like that lying around."

Edda was about to argue the point then realized it was useless. She knew she hadn't left anything lying around, but the evidence pointed to the contrary. "My mistake. Thank you for taking the time to answer my questions."

"No problem, Miss Case. You take care now."

After the two EMTs left Edda returned her attention to the window. Why was David up at two o'clock? Was he spying on her? Was he being more than just her friend? There were so many questions and next-to-no answers.

Chapter Five

"David?" The emotional atmosphere in the car was positively freezing.

David kept his eyes firmly fixed on the road.

"I'm sorry." How many times had she said that in the last two days? She had jumped down his throat when he turned up carrying an overnight bag with her toiletries, nightgown, and clothes. She didn't like people interfering and she told him so…again. Now it was about mending bridges.

"It's okay."

No, it wasn't okay. She could hear the hurt in his voice. "No, it's not. It was my fault."

"No, I understand. I should have asked first."

"If you'd done that, you would've been bringing me the bag as I was being discharged. I jumped to conclusions that I had no right jumping to."

David pulled the car over to the curb. "What conclusions?"

Edda stared out the window. "Never mind."

"No," he grabbed her hand, "I want to know."

"How did you know I was hurt?"

"I saw you in the backyard knocked out cold."

"You couldn't have known, unless you were looking over the fence. There was no light on. It was dark." How was he going to take her statement?

"No, I suppose I couldn't. Does it matter?"

"It shouldn't, but the fact that you don't want to answer is an answer in itself."

"I was outside having a smoke."

"And?"

"And I saw the back door open."

Edda doubted that. Their backyards backed onto an open paddock. The only light available would have been the moon. She pursed her lips.

"Okay, I was spying on you. Happy now?" He bit his lip and turned his gaze to the view outside.

"Why?" A dozen scenarios flew through her mind.

"The neighborhood kids can be a little rough at times. They like to play practical jokes."

"A shovel left for me to step on is not a practical joke."

"It is if they think you're gay, or something."

"What do you care?"

"I just didn't want to see you get hurt."

"A bit late for that."

"Yeah. Too late. Still, it was just as well that I found you."

"Which brings me back to my original question. Why? Why are you so interested in me? You know very well that I'm not interested, so there's got to be something more."

"I just want to be your friend."

"Uh-huh."

"We can help each other. If the neighbors see us as a couple then hopefully the kids will leave us alone."

David was running the conversation around in circles. Edda could sense there was something else driving David to stay close to her.

"I see your point. We're a couple, but not a 'couple.'" Edda lifted her fingers and bent them in air quotes as she said 'couple.'

"I can live with that." David started the engine and put the car in gear. He was in a better mood now and seemed satisfied that the matter was settled. Edda, on the other hand, only had more questions.

"Now, how did you get into my house?"

"I found your keys, then your cat. I figured both were safer in my pocket."

It made perfect sense when he told it, then why did she doubt him? The image of Jasper trying vainly to scramble out of David's jeans pocket brought a wry smile to her lips. At least there was one thing to laugh about.

Edda finally walked in the door and breathed deeply. It was good to be home, or as much as home could be in someone else's house. She put down her overnight bag next to the front door and waved to David, watching as he drove the car next door. Quickly she removed the key from the lock and closed the door before he took her curiosity as an invitation into her house.

"Jasper?" Edda looked around for her delinquent feline but he seemed to be missing. "Where are you, cat?" She checked every room downstairs then made sure all the doors were locked. Climbing the stairs would be exhausting and she wasn't coming down again any time soon. If the cat wasn't there then he could sit outside until she was ready to let him in.

The cat lay curled up in the middle of her bed, blissfully unaware of her return. "You lazy thing. Probably didn't even miss me." Her energy flagged and she slipped off her shoes, taking her place beside the cat and dozing off to sleep.

A sharp jab of pain woke her. Jasper had moved and was now snuggled next to her face, his paw resting across the bridge of her nose. Gently she lifted the paw and shifted it out of the way as it was a painful reminder of what had happened to her. David had said neighborhood kids were responsible. She hadn't seen any kids lurking around, just dear old David. Why would he lie about that? More to the point, why would he play such a cruel practical joke on her? But David didn't seem the type of person who would inflict damage on someone as a joke. She thought she was a better judge of character than that.

Edda knew she couldn't go back to sleep while her nose throbbed, so she decided to get up and go in search of her caffeine fix. It took more energy than she thought possible to descend the stairs and make her way to the kitchen. She looked out of the kitchen window as the coffeemaker made her addiction of choice, gazing across the field to the copse of trees and the cemetery on the far side. Gingerly, she walked outside and stared at the spot where she fell.

She examined the ground closely for any sign of the incident. The shovel was gone and the only evidence of the incident was a small spray of blood on the grass. She assumed that David made sure the shovel was out of the way so there was no repeat of the accident.

"Hey there, stranger."

Edda jumped. David leaned over the fence, cigarette in hand.

"You must be a pack-a-dayer."

"Not really, but the hospital thing went on for a few hours."

That was true. Getting discharged from the hospital was no longer a matter of just walking out the door. There was paperwork, scripts to fill, a doctor's approval, settling the bill, and finally cleaning up her mess and taking it home.

Edda took a seat. The effort of just getting up from bed had drained her and she felt a little light-headed.

"Are you okay?"

"I'm fine. Just a little tired."

"Do you want me to get some takeout?"

Edda didn't say a thing. David was killing her with kindness. "Look—"

"I'll order it for you. What do you want?"

She was tempted to say "nothing" but she figured he wouldn't leave her alone until she had something. "Chinese. Moo shu pork."

"Coming right up." He finished his cigarette. She heard him shuffle around and she assumed he had trodden on the butt to put it out. David disappeared into his house and Edda looked up at the sky. The blue had turned to a rosy hue as the sun set behind the trees in the distance. She took a deep breath and let it out slowly. What was she going to do about David? Short of going back home she was stuck with him.

"It'll be ready in fifteen minutes."

His voice broke the silence she had been enjoying. She opened her eyes and looked at him.

"What?" he asked.

"Nothing."

He shifted uncomfortably under her gaze. "Do you feel up to checking out the cemetery in the morning?"

"Are you still on vacation?"

"I go back next Monday."

That left Edda with three days of his constant attention. She felt sorry for the woman who would eventually catch him or, more to the point, let him catch her. Edda chuckled.

"What?"

"I was wondering what you would be like as an expectant dad." Yes, she felt very sorry indeed.

"What brought that up?"

"Nothing. It was just a random thought." After the earlier frostiness, she wanted to keep her thoughts to herself. "I didn't find the shovel."

"I put it away. I didn't want to have to visit you in the hospital again."

"I meant to thank you for looking after Jasper."

"Jasper? Oh, the cat. He came scratching at my leg when I was about to lock up the house. I couldn't let the poor thing starve."

"Thanks. I think you spoiled him though. He's gotten lazy."

"Nah, he probably misses you and wanted a cuddle."

"Probably."

The conversation dried up and they rested in companionable silence. Edda lazed on the deck chair while David draped his arms over the top of the fence. About fifteen minutes later David looked at his watch. "Dinner should be here soon." He glanced at the road and saw a car pull up. "Right on time."

After he left to answer the door, Edda shuddered. While she didn't mind eating dinner with him, she just wasn't up to company right now. The sun was setting and her nose ached. Despite her reluctance to take analgesics it seemed she would need to do just that to get some sleep. She looked up and saw David back at the fence, a plastic bag in his hand.

Edda rose slowly and felt the pressure in her head. There was a twinge of pain and she frowned.

Edda took the bag and looked inside. There was only enough for one. "Ummm, are you…?" She left the sentence hanging.

"Mine's inside. I figured you weren't up to company tonight." He handed over a business card. "That's got my cell number on it. If there's an emergency just call. I'll check on you in the morning."

Edda suddenly felt very guilty for thinking evil thoughts. Just when she thought she had David pegged he changed the game plan. The man was making it very hard for her to keep at a distance. "What do I owe you?"

"Don't worry about it."

"But—"

"When you're better you can make me dinner."

"David—"

"As a friend, Edda. Okay?"

She sighed. He had cornered her. "Okay." She was too tired to argue.

✝

Edda had managed to get a day's reprieve after she woke up sore and sorry. David took pity on her and allowed her some privacy, short-lived as it was. Unfortunately, the next morning came around all too quickly.

"How do we get to the field?"

"There's a path about half a mile down the street." David set off from his house in that direction and left Edda to trot along after him.

"What's the hurry?"

"You need longer legs, my girl."

Edda stopped in her tracks. Her eyebrow rose and her fists moved to her hips. "Girl?"

"Sure, don't you know about the birds and the bees? I'm a boy and you're a girl." He started to walk off when he added, "Of course, being so short and all, maybe you can't tell the difference."

49

"Why…why…you!" Edda started off after him but slowed down after a couple of steps. Her stamina, and her nose, was not what it was a few days ago. "Wait up!"

David stopped and waited for Edda to catch up. He slung his arm over her shoulder. "Come on, sleepyhead, let's go check this out."

The walk severely tested Edda's strength. By the time they had reached the copse of trees she was exhausted. David hesitated and reluctantly followed Edda to the rise. "It's a cemetery."

"I have to sit down." Edda took the few extra steps to a tree trunk and slumped to the ground. Her nose throbbed with the effort and she had to summon more strength to cover up the discomfort from David. Finally, she let out a sigh and allowed her legs to stretch out in front of her. "It really is pretty here," she commented.

David sat down next to her and stared at her. "It's a cemetery," he repeated.

"I know that, but it's still pretty. Wouldn't you like to spend the rest of eternity looking out over this view?"

"But it's a cemetery."

"You said that. Twice."

"And I'll say it again. It's a cemetery. Cemeteries are not pretty. They're tolerated at best."

Edda shrugged. "If you say so. How old is this place?"

"I'm not sure. I heard it had been relocated here."

"Where from?" Edda gazed at where she thought her house was. No, it wasn't her house. It was Lesley's house.

"Don't know. Does it matter?"

"I suppose not." Edda turned her attention to the gravestones. "Are there any ghost stories about this place?"

"Don't tell me that! Now I won't sleep at night."

"Is big bad David scared of ghosties?"

"Ghosties, zombies, vampires, you name it I don't like it."

"You must really love Halloween."

"If I can avoid it I will."

"Hah! Wait until next October, I'll…" Edda stopped short. Would she still be here then?

"Planning on staying a while?" he said then chuckled.

"It's not up to me."

"Sure it is. I'm sure Lesley can accommodate you."

"But I've got work to do and all my things are there."

"Petty excuses."

"I suppose they are." Edda hadn't really thought that far ahead.

"Surely, in your line of work you can send it in from here."

"I suppose I could." She had been mentally cursing David yesterday and yet this morning she was considering staying. Could she? Would she? Did she? Didn't she? Edda finally decided to be undecided about it.

David stood and extended his hand. "Enough lazing about, Miss Case." He grabbed her hand and pulled slowly, mindful of her injury. "Let's go home and I'll brew you a coffee."

She could almost smell it. "You're on."

"Did you find what you were looking for?"

"Not really." Edda scuffed her feet over the bed of fallen leaves and cast a cursory glance over the mass of gravestones. There was no obvious disturbance of the ground. Maybe someone was taking a shortcut through the cemetery at night. Then again, maybe she had imagined it all.

They walked back casually, taking their time along the overgrown track back to the street. Edda glanced over her shoulder at the group of trees on the small rise that protected the quaint cemetery. It made an interesting picture.

The stroll back to David's house was uneventful. The sun was shining and the birds were singing. It was going to be a beautiful day.

David lengthened his stride and arrived at the front door before she did. He opened the door and stood out of the way as Edda powered her way up the path and into his house. She heard him chuckle as she passed him.

"Where's my coffee?"

His chuckle became a laugh. "I can make instant if you're in that much of a hurry."

"Maybe I'll have both." He looked at her. "It's probably a little greedy."

"I'll keep you occupied with some breakfast while it brews."

"Can I use your bathroom?"

"Sure. Up the stairs. I'm sure you'll find it."

Edda dragged her tired body up the stairs and found the bathroom easily. After all, his house was the mirror image of hers. It seemed the houses in the estate were all basically the same.

As she washed up Edda looked at herself in the mirror. She knew the bruises there intimately because she studied them carefully when she came out of hospital. Now there was also a touch of pink on her cheeks from the sun.

Out of curiosity, she looked out the window toward the cemetery. The angle was much the same as hers, so David could have easily seen the light if he'd been awake.

Why was it bothering her so much? What was the big deal about seeing a light? David seemed to think it was kids, so why couldn't she just accept it as fact?

"Everything okay?" David's voice rose from the kitchen.

"Yes! Down in a minute!" She wondered if he was worried she had fainted or something. With one last look at the field, Edda shook her head and left her concerns behind.

The smell of brewing coffee filled the air. "Is it ready yet?" She took her seat and watched David making pancakes. "You're hopeful. David, if you keep feeding me like this I won't fit into the clothes I brought with me."

"Edda, honey, you have a long way to go before you reach that stage." He flipped the pancakes he had made. "Can you get the maple syrup?"

"Sure. Where is it?"

"Fridge door."

Edda stepped over to the refrigerator and opened it. She pulled out the bottle and put it on the table.

"Here you go." David put down a plate covered in pancakes.

"You have got to be joking!"

"They're not all for you, silly." He wiped his hands on a towel then sat down opposite her. "Dig in."

Edda helped herself to a pancake, adding a liberal amount of maple syrup on top. She had never indulged in a breakfast like this, but David had a way of awakening her taste buds. He was making sure she didn't starve herself.

He did have a point. Now that she was cooking for one she tended to cut corners on healthy eating, or not eating at all. It seemed like too much effort.

The coffee dripped noisily into the coffeepot and Edda's head rose. "Is it ready?" she asked hopefully.

"I'll give it to you even if it isn't."

"Sorry. I'm not human until I have my coffee."

"Okay, so what are you now?"

"A lesbian on the edge."

"Yikes!" David hurried the coffee and placed the mug in front of Edda then stepped back. "Go for it." Edda glared at him and he laughed.

As soon as the first mouthful of coffee passed her lips and started its journey down to her stomach Edda sighed. "Thanks."

"You're welcome." He sat down and continued his eating. "What's on the agenda for today?"

"The same as yesterday and the day before. Nothing."

"Edda—"

"Before you say anything, I know I need to keep myself busy. I'm too tired at the moment."

"That's an excuse, and you know it."

Edda knew he was right.

"How about I show you where the supermarket is? There's a handy little shopping center nearby but it's a little hard to find."

She was happy to accept David's change of subject. "You just want to see the contents of my shopping basket."

"Not unless you're secretly hoarding Oreos."

"And they're your weakness?"

David looked sheepishly at her. "They could be."

"Uh-huh."

"I plead the Fifth." He stood and carried their plates to the sink. "How about you go home and make a list and we'll go shopping."

That cinched it. David was definitely gay. No man worth his gender would willingly go shopping. "Fine." Edda stood and moved to David. "Thanks." She grabbed his hand and squeezed it.

"Is half an hour enough?"

"It should be."

"I'll come and get you."

"Until then." Edda left his house and walked briskly back to her front door. It seemed that David was making himself indispensable.

Chapter Six

Ten minutes later the doorbell rang. Was it David again so soon? She shuffled to the door and opened it.

"Hello."

"Errr…hello." It wasn't David.

"Do you remember me?"

"You're the nurse at the hospital. Did I forget something?"

"No. I just thought I'd call by."

Edda blinked a couple of times to clear her mind. "Come in." She stood back and allowed Delia to enter. "I wasn't expecting company." Edda led the way through to the kitchen and put the kettle on. "Would you like a coffee?"

"Do you have tea?"

Edda opened a cupboard or two before she found a box. "I'm afraid there are only teabags." She tried not to look for a use-by date.

"That's fine."

Edda reached for the cups and saucers.

"A mug will do," Delia said as she sat down at the table.

Edda looked over her shoulder and Delia smiled at her.

"Are you all right?"

"Fine, why?"

"You're frowning." Delia stood and moved over to where Edda stood. She studied her nose intently, leaving Edda to stare at the woman.

She has nice eyes, Edda decided. They were the sort of eyes that reminded her of those pools of water in the depths of a forest. Dark and seemingly calm on the surface, but one knew there was a fierce undercurrent underneath.

"Sorry, it's the nurse in me." Delia backed away and sat down again.

After the kettle boiled Edda sat down in a chair opposite her visitor and pushed the mug of tea across the table. She left the sugar and milk on the table for Delia to help herself.

"Can I ask why you're here? Do you normally make it your job to follow up on your patients?"

"I understand you have no immediate family close by. I just wanted to make sure you were all right. You were a bit woozy when you were discharged and I was concerned that you might have another accident without someone to keep an eye on you."

Delia sipped her tea a while before she spoke again. "The fellow who was with you—"

"David."

"David. He's your neighbor?"

Edda nodded gently and took a sip of her coffee. "I'm fine. Really. David gave me his cell number in an emergency. He's only next door." To her, it seemed a flimsy excuse for a visit. Did this woman think she had made a connection with her? She was now having second thoughts about staying around, because if everyone she met acted like this she was going to be mobbed by people wanting to be her friend.

Edda caught a glimpse of the nurse's uniform underneath Delia's coat. "Are you on your way to work or on your way home?"

"I beg your pardon?"

"The uniform."

"Ahh. I go on duty in about an hour. I just wanted to make sure there was someone to keep an eye on you for the next few days."

"I go back for a checkup on Monday."

"That's good." Delia sipped her tea as Jasper casually strode into the room. "Your cat. What is his name?"

"Jasper."

"Yes, Jasper. Hello, kitty kitty kitty." Delia extended her hand and the cat took two steps toward her then stopped. He hissed at her and ran away.

"I'm so sorry. Normally he's a very friendly cat." Edda looked in the direction the cat had taken and wondered what had caused such a response.

"Never mind." Delia took one more sip of her tea then stood. "Well, I must be off." She grabbed her bag and waited for Edda to join her.

"Well, thank you for dropping by. I'll be fine. Believe me, David is keeping an eagle eye on me."

"That's good to hear."

Edda led her back to the front door and opened it. "Thank you, Delia, for your concern."

"You're most welcome." Delia extended her hand for Edda to take. It was warm and firm. Delia smiled at her and the smile extended up to her eyes. Jasper came up and wound his body around Edda's legs, purring and rubbing against her. He stopped, looked up at Delia and growled. "I'm leaving," Delia announced.

"I don't know what's wrong with this cat."

"Don't worry about it. Here's my card. If you have any difficulties you can give me a call. Goodbye." Delia turned and walked briskly down the path to her car.

Edda looked down at the cat. "What's got you so bent out of shape, huh?" Jasper looked up at her and meowed. "You say that now. You could have been nice to her." He meowed again and went back to rubbing his head against her trousers. There was the sound of a horn and Edda raised her hand to wave goodbye. When the car disappeared from sight she closed the door. "Now I wonder what that was all about?" She took the card to the kitchen and left it by the refrigerator.

Five minutes later David pounded on the front door. "Are you ready?" he hollered.

Edda really hadn't had the chance to make a list but she figured that she would need most things. She grabbed her purse and walked out into the sunlight, locking up before she left. "Let's go."

†

David was right. It was a little tricky to get to the shopping center. There was an odd turn or two that she tried to put to memory, but she felt sure that her first solo trip would be hit and miss. He warned her about a local convenience store, telling her the owner would rob her blind if she didn't know the real price of the items. Edda thought David was really sweet. He was taking his responsibilities seriously.

David helped to carry the numerous sacks of groceries into the house. She had probably gone overboard with the amount of food, but she didn't want to go shopping again any time soon. The rather large scratching post for Jasper was placed prominently in the lounge room, but she suspected that it was probably too late for Jasper's need to stretch his claws.

"Damn it!"

"What?" David emerged from the kitchen.

Edda picked up some letters sitting on the table. "I should have posted these to Lesley."

"Here, I'll post them for you." He grabbed the small pile of mail out of her hand. She wasn't quite sure what to do with Lesley's mail so she'd decided to forward it on. In due course she would expect her own set of mail.

"Is there much more?"

"A couple more sacks and I'll leave you to unpack."

She was tired. Had David picked up on that? Probably, otherwise he would have offered to help her. David passed her in the hallway with the last two sacks. A moment later he passed her again and kept going out the door and down the path.

"Thanks, David!"

"You're welcome!"

She closed the door and sighed, feeling all of her fifty-two years. Edda trudged into the kitchen and surveyed the sea of paper sacks. "What was I thinking?"

It took half an hour to find homes for all the cans, boxes, frozen goods, and fresh fruit. It had been exhausting and it was time to treat herself to a coffee. While she sipped it her mind wandered.

A gentle brush against her leg caught her attention and she looked down. "What have you been up to?" Jasper meowed at her and turned his body to brush his other side against her leg. He looked up expectantly, crouched for a second then sprang up onto her lap. Before Edda had a chance to protest, he settled down and waited for her hand to touch his fur.

"Don't get too comfortable." Edda finished her coffee. With no immediate plans, she decided a nap was in order. Carrying Jasper upstairs, Edda slipped off her shoes and settled down on the bedcovers. Before she even acknowledged where Jasper had settled her eyes closed.

†

The next morning David lay in wait for her. As soon as she stepped out the front door, he appeared. "You took your time."

"I didn't know I was on a schedule." She looked at him dubiously as she joined him and began to walk. "You're taking this 'couple' thing a little too seriously." She added a smile to take the sting out of her words.

"Well, Miss Case, I'm finding that you are a fascinating woman and I'd like to get to know you better."

"David—"

"Yeah, I know. A lost cause. But I'd still like to get to know you."

Edda shook her head. "I don't live here, David. I'm only staying—"

"But that could change," he pleaded.

She stopped walking. "Why?" He simply shrugged his shoulders. It seemed he couldn't explain it either.

"Where are we going today?" Edda let the subject drop, writing the experience up to one of those unexplainable things like déjà vu and clairvoyance. Maybe one day he'd know too.

"Come on," he said, gently tugging her hand. "The sooner we get this over, the sooner you can have your coffee."

He said the word coffee like it was a magical incantation. Maybe it was. Edda's eyes lit up with the thought of a hot, brewed coffee. It was enough incentive for her to put some effort into her walking.

She was surprised to find he led her back to the cemetery. "Why are we back here?"

"I suppose proving to myself that I can overcome my fears."

The patch of ground seemed the same as it had been the day before. Well, nearly. Her finger rubbed over the top of one of the headstones, its waxy feel sliding easily over her tip. She brought her finger to her nose and smelled it. "Wax." She glanced around the headstones and felt a shiver run up her spine. Something wasn't right. Now was not the time to mention it.

David looked over her shoulder. "Probably kids. They come here to make out. Probably light a candle or two to make it not so dark."

"Whatever happened to the backseat of the boy's car?"

"Do you think any father is going to be looking for his daughter in a graveyard?"

"If everyone knows this is a popular make-out spot, why not?"

"Probably for the same reason I wouldn't come here at night."

"All the more reason to make sure she's safe. Any father would want to protect his daughter not only from the boy but from any unsavory types lurking around."

"Unsavory types?" David laughed.

"What?"

"You sound like one of those romance novels."

"Why, sir, do you doubt my intentions?" She smiled sweetly at him, and it made him laugh harder.

"That's better," he said. "It's really nice to see you smile."

Edda nodded and let her smile drop.

"Oh no, don't lose it. It lights up your face." His hand brushed her cheek.

"David…" she warned.

"Just let me fuss, okay? You need a bit of pampering."

"You have been pampering me to within an inch of my life, David. Any more and I may explode."

"And that's a bad thing?" He started down the small incline to the pathway leading to the street. "Come on, I think coffee is calling you."

Edda looked around one final time and followed David along the path. She restrained herself from looking back, even though she felt someone, or something, was watching her.

†

"Not bad." He took the last bite of his own breakfast. "Nearly as good as me." He made it sound like a challenge, but she wasn't going to bite on his obvious baiting.

Edda held the mug in her hands, taking a heartfelt swallow of the brew. "Coffee's great."

"Yeah?"

"What? You don't like it?"

"Sure. I didn't mean anything by that. I've never seen anyone swoon over coffee before."

"I do not swoon, or weep, or jump for joy. I appreciate a good cup of coffee." She carelessly took another swig of coffee and bumped her nose with the mug. She barely kept herself from dropping the coffee, but she did manage to put it back on the table. "Shit!" The word escaped her mouth before she could censor herself. At that particular moment she didn't care.

"Oh, God! Are you all right?" David stood and hovered over her, hopping from one foot to the other like an ecstatic puppy.

"Yeah, I'll live." Despite the good breakfast and the company, Edda felt depressed. Life was kicking her while she was down.

"Do you want something for the pain?"

Her face must have told a story.

"Look…" She saw David's expression drop. "I think I'll go home and lie down. If that's okay with you."

"Of course." He reached for Edda's forearm to help her up.

"David. I have a broken nose, not a broken leg. Okay?"

"Oh." He pulled back abruptly. "Yeah. Sure."

Edda stood and immediately felt the painful pressure on her nose. Now she wished she had let David help her. She had told him she was fine so now she had to live with it. He escorted her to the front door.

Edda stepped through the door before turning to face him. "David? Thanks." She gave him a smile and wandered down the short pathway to the street. She could feel his gaze on her as she walked next door and disappeared through the front door. He would make all those doting mothers out there proud.

Before she had a chance to lay on the bed her cell rang. There were only three possibilities as to who was on the other end of the line—her mother, Tamara, or Lesley. It would be an even call as to which one it was.

She retrieved her phone. "Hello?"

"Edda?" It was Tamara. "So good to hear your voice, honey. How are you?"

"Fine. What can I do for you?" There was a hesitation in the conversation. "Tamara?"

"Yeah? Oh…yeah. I wouldn't be bothering you otherwise, but I got a call from Daniel…Daniel Rosetti. He was asking if you were available for a couple of specials. I told him he may be out of luck, but he asked me to ask you as a favor. Feel free to say no."

Was she ready to work? Edda looked around the bedroom to reinforce where she was. "I don't know, Tam. I really don't know."

"Okay, I'll call him back."

It seemed that Tamara had made the decision for her. "Wait. Can you send me the details and specifications and I'll take a look. I'll give him my decision once I've seen what the project is."

"That was a better answer than I thought it would be. I was sure you'd say no."

"That might still be the answer, but I'd like to take a look first."

"I'll send Karen with it. Give me your address." Edda gave it. "Wow! That's going to be an overnight trip."

"Send it by courier, Tam. Don't drag poor Karen out for this trip."

"Is there anything else you need?"

"All my stuff is at the apartment. I'll call Lesley to let her know a courier will be by to pick up the box. You can send that along with the envelope," she said, envisioning the large yellow envelope Daniel always sent containing project information. "I'll expect the courier in a day or so."

"Ye-ah. I'll hear from you."

The line went dead and Edda looked at the cell in her hand. Knowing Tamara's almost-paranoid need for security, she would be expecting Karen tomorrow.

Moments after hanging up she had second thoughts. Was she ready? Should she be? She was confused by what she was supposed to feel. What she really needed was someone to talk to; someone who didn't have a vested interest in her. David would use his considerable persuasive power to convince her to get back to work, but she wasn't sure whether she was ready to hear it.

The only other person she knew was Delia. She went in search of Delia's business card. Only after an increasingly frantic search did she discover where she had left it—sitting in plain sight next to the refrigerator. She wouldn't dare mention her lack of memory in front of Delia in case she was dragged back into hospital for another CT scan. Revealing anything about her health seemed to result in her being pushed and prodded to within an inch of her life.

†

As she suspected, Karen, her personal assistant, arrived the next afternoon. The small Honda Civic roared up the driveway, and Karen revved the engine to make sure everyone knew she had arrived.

Edda looked through the front window and could see her bounding out of the car and bouncing her way up to the front door. She counted to three then held up her finger as the pounding on the door started. "Hey! Edda! Come on, sweet cheeks!"

Edda winced. Somehow 'sweet cheeks' just didn't work in this community. She raced to the door and flung in open. "Will you keep it quiet!" she hissed. One or two of the neighbors emerged from their houses to see what the noise was about. "Do you want me to get thrown out of here?"

"What the hell happened to you?"

"An accident. I walked into a door in the dark. You know how it is."

"Uh-huh." Karen's response left Edda nervous. She wasn't fooling anyone, but the truth was just too…stupid or unbelievable…to mention. She couldn't decide which description was suitable for her situation, so she settled for a white lie instead.

"Come inside." Edda all but pushed her inside.

"What's the hurry?" Karen looked at her over her shoulder.

"Nothing. Why stand out in the street when we could be inside enjoying a coffee?"

"Uh-huh."

Those words again. Edda decided that her lying skills were just not up to Karen's scrutiny. "Did you have a good trip?"

"Not bad. What was that all about out there?"

"Karen, this is not the big city, okay? People are a little more…"

"Bigoted?"

"Selective," Edda amended. "I'm just not up to the fight right now. Get your things and I'll show you to your room."

"Cool." Karen seemed unaffected by her ever-so-slight rebuff. "I've got stuff from Tamara. She's finally losing it, you know."

Edda seriously doubted that. While Tamara could get stressed out over deadlines, she had a long way to go before she, as Karen put it, 'lost it.' "How so?"

"There was no way she was sending this with a courier. No, I had to schlep my way out here to give it to you personally."

"It's not unheard of."

"I know…but I had plans. She wasn't going to take no for an answer."

"You knew this might happen."

Karen sighed. "Yeah, I know. But I had plans, you know."

"Peter?"

"Danny."

"What happened to Peter?"

Karen shrugged. She changed boyfriends like other people changed clothes.

"That was quick."

"Sometimes it's like that. Anyway, here's her majesty's parcel delivered safe and sound." She handed over the large envelope.

"Any trouble picking up the box from my apartment?"

"Nope. Ready as promised. It's in the trunk."

"Where's your bag?"

Karen looked uncomfortable. "I…err…it's still in the car. I thought I'd stop in at a hotel on the way home."

"Nonsense, after coming all this way I can at least offer you a bed for the night."

"A bed??" Karen's voice rose a notch. "No, that's not necessary."

Edda looked at her, perplexed. "What is the matter with you?" When Karen couldn't look her in the eye she knew. "The guest bedroom, you dummy! You could always sleep on the sofa if you want, but I won't promise that Jasper won't sit on your face. Did you think…?"

"Nnooooo." But both of them knew it was a lie. "Well maybe, but…" her words trailed off. Edda suspected that Karen knew she was digging herself a bigger hole.

"I'm in mourning, for Christ's sake!" Edda said. "Besides you're too young for my taste."

"What's that supposed to mean?" Karen planted her fists on her hips. "I'm not good enough? Too young to be experienced?"

"Whoa!" Edda held up her hands. "What are you getting upset for? We're never going to be in that position to find out. Get your bag. You are staying in the guest room, and that's final. I'll even give you a chair to put behind the door, okay?"

Karen turned and walked out to her car.

Edda could feel her heart racing. Was Karen just tired or was she showing something of herself that Edda hadn't seen before? She'd known the girl for three years without so much as a harsh word from her. Well…there was the occasional expletive, but she was also guilty of that. No, Karen had never shown any problem with Edda's sexual orientation. Then again, she'd never had to stay overnight in her apartment either. For a fleeting moment she thought of playing a prank on her then thought better of it. She couldn't afford to lose an assistant right now.

A rather subdued Karen reentered the house and stood at the bottom of the staircase with an overnight bag. She looked suitably chastised. "Sorry, I overreacted."

Edda smiled. "Come on. I'll show you to your room." She climbed the stairs and stood outside the guest bedroom. "Here you go." She turned the knob and opened the door. "If there's anything you need I'm just down the hall. Next room, in fact." Edda twitched one eyebrow. She couldn't help herself.

"No, I'm sure it'll be fine." Karen was skittish as a newborn foal. Edda kind of liked it. Karen was always outgoing and brash, confident of herself and her abilities nearly to the point of arrogance. It was refreshing to see her shaken up a little.

Edda retrieved a couple of towels from the linen closet and handed them over. "If you want to have a shower or clean up." Edda then disappeared into her own room and came back with a chair. "As promised." She carried it into the guestroom and stepped out. "Dinner will be in a couple of hours."

Karen stood there, her mouth opening and closing without sound. "Ah…thanks." She escaped into the sanctuary that was the guestroom.

Edda stood there and chuckled. "Strange girl," she whispered.

Chapter Seven

The next morning there was a knock on the front door, and Edda was quick to respond. "Hi, come in."

"I was surprised to get your call." Delia stepped into the house.

"I was kind of surprised myself." Edda led the way through to the kitchen. "Tea?"

"Thanks." Delia sat down on the same chair she had sat on days before.

Edda could feel Delia's gaze on her back and she mentally squirmed. What had possessed her to call the woman? Silently she placed the tea in front of Delia before she sat down to nurse her own coffee. "So."

"So." Delia looked at her and smiled.

She has beautiful eyes. The thought again popped into Edda's head. "You said to call."

Delia took a sip of her tea. "That I did."

The conversation was already uncomfortable and Edda questioned her decision to contact Delia in the first place.

"What's wrong?" It seemed Delia had decided to start the ball rolling.

"I…" Edda took a deep breath and spoke, "I don't want to be happy."

"You don't?" Delia put down her mug. "Why not?"

"June died. I'm in mourning."

"Who's June?"

Crap. Edda hadn't mentioned June before. "June is…was my partner," she said quietly.

"Oh."

That one word said everything. "It's okay. You don't have to stay." Edda studied her mug like it held the secret of the universe. She only hoped that Delia didn't call down the wrath of God on her.

"You want me to go?"

Edda wasn't sure what made her look up. Maybe it was the intonation in the words. "I thought…"

"You're obviously used to a negative reaction to that news."

"Yes, and it's not very pleasant. I just keep the identity of my partner neutral to avoid confrontations."

Delia lifted her mug to her lips and took another mouthful. "And you don't want to be happy. Why?"

"Like I said, I'm in mourning. I don't want to feel anything but sadness."

"And you feel other things?"

"Not sadness."

"And when do you feel this?"

"David is a big cause of that."

"David. He was the one who visited you."

"Yes. I've only been here for a couple of weeks. He's decided he has to be my best friend."

"And you don't want him to be."

"Yes! No. I don't know. I feel guilty."

"Guilty."

"Yes, guilty." Edda stood up and paced. "I don't want to feel anything. I don't want to be interested, or amused, or make friends. I don't want to feel joy."

"Why did you move?"

"Pardon?" Edda stopped pacing.

"Why did you move? You said you've only been in this place for a short time."

"I did a house swap with Lesley. She's the one who owns this place. I wanted to get away."

"You wanted to escape the sad memories in your house. You've done that and now you're complaining?" Delia studied her. "You can't have it both ways."

"She was my life."

"In your heart that won't change. Why are you afraid to live?"

"I loved her very much. I'm sure I'm not supposed to feel anything but pain."

"But you feel you want to do something?"

"I suppose that's it. I feel an itch to get back to work."

"Then don't let that stop you. It may sound callous, but life goes on whether you decide to stop or not. I'm sure June would want you to get on with your life."

"I know she would, but that doesn't make me feel any less guilty."

"Hey, it's not like you're jumping back into a relation—" Delia's sentence broke off as Karen wandered into the kitchen dressed in extremely short shorts and a crop top. Delia kept quiet but Edda felt the heat of her gaze.

"Err, Karen. Hi."

"Hi Edda," Karen said brightly.

"Sleep well?" Edda was sure a blush was slowly creeping up her face.

"Sure did."

"No unwanted visitors?" She said this more for Delia than herself.

"Nope, the chair worked just fine." Karen opened the refrigerator and found an apple. "May I?" She held it up for Edda to inspect.

"Sure. Karen, this is Delia. Delia…Karen." Edda tried not to look at Delia's face, even though she knew exactly what she would find there.

"Hi there, Delia," Karen said as she started to walk out of the kitchen.

"Pleased to meet you, Karen."

Edda watched Karen disappear from sight. "I know what you're thinking."

"You probably do."

"You don't pull any punches, do you?"

"Oh, I pull plenty of them, but I'm not sure what to say here."

"Karen is my assistant. I got a call from Tamara, my agent. There was an urgent job and she sent Karen to deliver everything I need. Karen slept here overnight. Alone."

"Uh-huh. This explains the guilt then."

Edda didn't know whether Delia was disgusted with her or just being cheeky. "Nothing happened. She's not my type. Besides, she's twenty years younger than I am."

"That wouldn't stop some people I know."

"Why am I justifying myself to you?" Edda's voice rose.

"Because you were the one who called me, remember?"

Edda sat down in her chair and lifted her hands to her face. "God, it's all a mess."

"No, it's not." Delia stood up and moved to Edda's chair. "Come here." She extended her arms and welcomed her.

Edda cried. This was the first time she shared her sorrow with another woman over June's death. Her body shook and

Delia's hand slowly stroked her back. "Everything will be all right," Delia whispered.

"Y-Y-You can't p-p-promise that." Edda pulled back and looked at her.

"No, I can't, but time is a great healer."

Edda leaned into Delia's comforting embrace and absorbed the warmth there. Her tears eventually subsided and she collected her wits.

"Excuse me." Both Edda and Delia glanced sideways to see Karen standing in the door. "Don't let me interrupt you."

"No! No, no, no," Edda backed away to put space between herself and Delia. "Don't be ridiculous! Nothing's going on." Her stuttering words did little to allay her fears.

"Uh-huh."

"Tell her, Delia. Tell her nothing's going on," Edda urged.

"What she says is true," Delia said.

"Fine." Karen passed them and threw the apple core into the garbage bin. She grabbed a glass and went to the fridge for milk. "If you don't mind, I'll be leaving in about an hour. I want to get home before dark."

"Thanks, Karen. Tell Tamara I'll be in touch by the end of the week to let her know my decision."

"So you're sticking around here a little while longer?"

"Looks like it." Edda made a mental note to call Lesley.

Edda watched Karen leave for the second time and knew what had just happened would be known through her various social circles in no time. "Look…" Edda turned her attention to Delia and stopped. "What's wrong?"

"Nothing," Delia said emotionlessly. "Nothing at all. I must be going."

"You haven't finished your tea."

"No, another time."

"Wait!" Edda reached out and grabbed Delia's wrist. "Stay. Tell me what's wrong." She went over the conversation in her head to try and find the cause of Delia's withdrawal.

"I can't. I have another appointment." Delia had already grabbed her handbag and was walking out of the kitchen. Edda was helpless but to follow her to the door.

"I suppose I'll talk to you soon."

"Maybe."

Edda opened the door and Delia left without another word. As she drove away, Edda had a bad feeling that she wouldn't be seeing Delia again.

"Sorry about that."

Edda turned to find Karen seated on the stairs.

"I didn't mean to interrupt anything."

"There was nothing to interrupt."

"Didn't look like that to me."

"June's death hit me and Delia was just comforting me. That's all it was."

"Are you trying to convince me or convince yourself?"

"Karen," Edda growled. "There is nothing going on. Do I make myself clear?"

"Does Delia know that?"

"Of course she knows that."

"Well, from where I stood, you were pushing her away. I suppose if I were in her position I'd take that as a slap in the face."

"She's not gay."

"Did she tell you that?"

"No, but we don't know each other well enough for that information to come out."

"Come out. Hah! Funny."

"Karen. Don't think you're indispensable."

"Come on, Edda. Who else would put up with you?"

Karen had a point. While Edda liked to think of herself as a perfectionist she knew others around her thought she was a pain in the ass.

"I'm not looking for another relationship."

"I never said you were."

Karen was beginning to annoy the hell out of her. "Karen, drop it. And I better not hear about it on the grapevine."

"Me?" Karen pointed at herself but she couldn't keep the grin off her face.

"I'm being serious here. It was all a mistake. Let's leave it that way."

"Fine, but don't blame me if you don't hear from her again." Karen stood and climbed the stairs.

Edda watched Karen's back. "You've got it all wrong," she muttered.

✝

An hour later Karen came down the stairs with her suitcase in hand and ready to leave. This time she was dressed more sensibly in jeans and T-shirt. There was not a hint of skin above, below or in between.

"Thanks, Karen, for coming out all this way."

"Tamara said it was top secret and she didn't want the couriers to, as she put it, 'get their grubby hands on it.' It got me out of a day's work, who am I to complain?" Karen's tell-it-like-it-is attitude got her fired from her last seven jobs. Luckily for Karen, Edda understood perfectly. She didn't suffer fools lightly either.

"I'll have a look over the proposal and see what I can do. I'll contact her later this week, all right?"

"Sure thing. Thanks for the hospitality."

"Maybe next time you can stay for a couple of days."

"Yeah? A fully paid holiday?"

Edda laughed. "Try to be subtle about it, okay?" Edda opened the door. "We'll see." She pushed Karen out and into the arms of David. "Oh."

"Sorry, I didn't know you were entertaining guests." David's arms wrapped around Karen's waist.

"Just business," Edda said.

"Really?" He stepped away and looked down into Karen's eyes. "Hi there. My name is David."

"David, Karen. Karen, David." Edda pushed harder to get them both off her front stoop.

"Karen, hello." David extended his hand and waited for Karen to take it.

"Hi." Karen reciprocated, her hand held firmly in David's. The shake went on…and on.

"Oh brother." Edda pushed harder. "Come on, Karen, time to go."

"I can spare a minute or two."

"David? What did you want?"

"I can't for the life of me remember. So, Karen, are you a friend of Edda's?"

"I'm her assistant."

"Really?" He started to stroke the back of Karen's hand. "Does that mean I'll be seeing you on a regular basis?"

"Never mind me," Edda muttered.

"Once or twice, I should think."

"Then I better not waste any time. Would you like to have my baby?"

Edda swallowed hard and started coughing. "You what?" She gasped for air as the saliva slid down her throat. "David! Are you nuts?"

"I'm not getting any younger," he said dreamily.

"Oh, for crying out loud. Get a room, both of you!" Edda realized what she had just said. "Scratch that. No room.

Karen, get in your car. David, back to your house." Edda wriggled in between the two of them and shoved them apart. "None of this lovey-dovey stuff."

"Edda! Can't you see that I've found the love of my life?"

"You just met her."

"I know. Isn't she great?"

"Snap out of it!" Edda was so tempted to smack the silly smile off his face. "Karen. Go home." Edda grabbed her keys and threw Karen's case into the trunk of the car. She unlocked the driver's side and pointed to the seat. "Karen. Sit." Karen stared at her. "Sit, Karen. Get in the damned car."

Karen gazed at David, then at Edda. Edda knew that look. She'd had it a few times with June, and her heart ached with the memory. David and Karen were experiencing what Edda had, and she was jealous.

"David! Unhand that girl." Finally David did as he was ordered. "Karen, for the last time, get in the car."

Karen reluctantly took the few steps to the car, all the while looking over her shoulder at David. Edda was tempted to put something in her way for her to bump into, but nothing was near at hand.

"Bye," Karen said sweetly, giving David a tiny wave with her fingers.

"Bye," David returned the silly wave.

Edda rolled her eyes.

Karen called David over to the car and planted a quick kiss on his lips. Karen slid into the driver's seat and reached into the glove compartment. She handed David a card. "Give me a call." He glanced at the card then returned his gaze to Karen before he nodded.

The engine revved loudly and Karen screeched out of the driveway. *"Ciao!"* she called.

"Yeah, yeah. One down, one to go." Edda grabbed David's elbow and steered him into her house. "Are you out of your mind?" She continued to push him until they were in the kitchen. "Sit."

"Don't you believe in love at first sight?"

"No."

"But you and June…"

"There's no such thing."

"What do you call what I feel for Karen?"

"Stupidity."

"That's not fair! Just because you're grieving doesn't mean I have to suffer."

Edda walked out of the kitchen and up the staircase. David's words cut her deep. He was right, of course, but that didn't stop the pain. She lay on her bed and looked at the framed picture sitting on the bedside table. It was one of her and June, smiling like there wasn't a care in the world. At that time there wasn't. It was perfect then.

Edda stood up and went to the closet. She found her bag and placed it on the bed. Inside was a photo album. As she flipped through the pages she remembered the events that shaped the images displayed there. Maybe David ought to see these.

She descended the stairs, album in hand, and prepared herself for an apology but the kitchen was empty. "Damn."

Edda put on her shoes, found her keys and left the house. It seemed she would have to make the first move.

She knocked on his front door. "David?" She knocked again. "Come on, David. Let me in." It started to sprinkle so Edda knocked a little harder. "It's starting to rain out here." Just when she thought he would leave her standing in the rain the door opened.

He glanced at her for a moment before his eyes looked at the ground. "What do you want?"

"You were in such a hurry to leave that you didn't get the whole story. Now, can I come in?" Silently he stepped aside to let her enter. "Nice place." She tried to sound upbeat because David had clammed up. "Decorate it yourself?"

"Coffee?" he said guardedly.

"Please." Edda watched him move around the kitchen and waited until he sat down opposite her with mug in hand. "David, I'm not trying to stop you seeing Karen, but I want you to look at it with a clear head."

"Edda, this has never happened to me before. It's got to be a sign."

"Please don't tell Karen what I'm about to tell you. As far as I'm aware the girl has never had a long-term relationship. In the time I've known her, the boyfriends only last a couple of months. The one with the most stamina lasted six months."

"What are you trying to say?"

"Karen may prove me wrong, and I hope for your sake she does, but the gloss wears off a new relationship pretty quickly with her. I don't want to see you hurt."

"I saw it in her eyes, Edda. She can't fool me."

"I'm not saying she's fooling you. She could very well feel 'this love at first sight' that you are so enamored about. But any relationship, especially a long-term one, takes work. Love doesn't pay the bills. Love doesn't cook the meals. Love doesn't settle the arguments."

"Is that what happened between you and June?"

He had brought the subject around to her. Maybe it was time to talk about it. "The first time we met it didn't go well."

"You hated her on sight?"

"Hate? No. She was someone I'd met at a party. It was all polite and everything but there was no immediate spark.

Hell, I didn't even know she was gay until our third meeting."

David chuckled lightly. Edda leaned over and patted his hand. He looked at her and smiled. Silent apologies were always the best, or so she thought.

"The love did come, after we had gotten to know one another." She opened the album. "A relationship is not easy. Love plays a big part, but it's not the only part. Compromise and patience are big factors, as is a large dose of humor. Loving someone you see three or four times a week for dinner or a date is completely different to living with someone twenty-four seven."

David stood up and moved to stand behind Edda so he could see the photos over her shoulder. Her finger hovered over the first photo in the book. "That was from the first meeting. We had a mutual friend who wanted some 'names' at her party," Edda said.

"And you were a 'name' even then?"

"I'd just begun. One of my bags was featured in a shoot for *Vogue*."

"Wow! I'm in the presence of a celebrity."

"Celebrity? Hah!" Her finger traced June's outline.

"What did June do?"

"She was an agent."

"Agent? As in actor's agent?"

"As in model's agent."

"I see a theme running through this story."

"Yes, my bag," Edda said. David laughed long and loud. Edda couldn't help herself; she smiled.

"There you go." His hand rested on her shoulder. She looked up into sympathetic eyes. "It's interesting to see the relationship progress in the photos. See? In the first one both of you are standing apart. The second one is a little closer and the third one you're together."

"The third one happened because the photographer pushed us together."

"And look what happened after that."

"It was more like look what happened in spite of that."

"What happened?"

"Everyone thought we were together."

"And what's wrong with that?"

"People I knew started asking for favors concerning June and vice versa. It was like our own personal Vietnam, and we weren't even seeing each other."

"Ouch!" David said in sympathy.

"But we became friends because of it. She was the only one who knew what I was going through. Ironically, we started seeing each other because people thought we were seeing each other."

"If you say so. I sort of got lost back at the favors."

"By the time we became lovers we were ready for it. We were good friends and we respected and trusted each other. We had the basic building blocks of a relationship in place before we got together. I'm not saying that you should do that, but don't rely on love alone."

"You seem a bit jaded about love."

"Jaded? Not necessarily. I've seen too many relationships break up based on love alone."

"That sounds jaded to me." David smiled.

"Fine. Believe what you will. Can you at least promise me something?"

"What?"

"Don't let her make all the decisions. Don't let her run the relationship."

He looked at her puzzled. "Err, okay."

"Compromise and patience, David. Take it slowly and make sure it's right for you."

"Like you did."

"I nearly missed out."

"I can see that you were very much in love." He pointed to a new photo. "What about this one?" It was a picture of the two of them on holiday, smiling at one another.

"That was the beginning of the end," she said with a heavy heart.

"What happened?"

"She had stomach pains. The doctor told her it was an ulcer and prescribed medication for it. After six months the pain got worse and she got a second opinion. Stage four stomach cancer. She went through the chemo but the prognosis didn't change."

"Did you sue the first doctor?"

"I visited him after the second diagnosis. When I told him what had happened I could see the fear in his eyes. It was then I realized we were as much at fault as he was. We should have gotten a second opinion right at the beginning."

"So what did you do?"

"I gave him a second chance, with a warning that if he screwed up again he would pay."

"You're awfully forgiving."

"Suing him wasn't going to bring June back. The only ones to benefit from that arrangement would be the lawyers."

"True, but it would have covered all the medical expenses."

"I suppose so. Money wasn't such an issue, and June had medical insurance. Finding someone to blame seemed pointless."

David remained silent. He laid his hand on Edda's shoulder as she turned the remaining pages that documented the rest of June's life. "We should have sought a second opinion," Edda repeated quietly. "Cancer is an ugly disease." She glanced at the last two photos in the album. "Toward the end she couldn't eat, and the morphine barely touched the pain." She closed the book. "Cancer is indiscriminate and unforgiving. I wouldn't wish it on anyone."

"I'm so sorry, hon." He squeezed her shoulder and she took the invitation for a good cry. Edda stood and stepped into David's welcoming arms. Again her tears fell unheeded. She wasn't sure how much time had passed but her body was tired. She had shed too many tears this day.

David urged her to sit. "Let me get lunch." Edda watched David move around the kitchen to collect the makings of a light meal.

"Why do you feel the need to protect me?" Edda hoped that her own revelation would bring about his.

"Protect you? I don't think—"

"David. Let's be fair about this. You are making it painfully clear that you want to protect me. What from? Or from whom?"

David stopped what he was doing and leaned heavily on the kitchen counter. "I was twelve when my brother died. I couldn't protect him. I want to make sure that doesn't happen again." He turned his head and looked out at the view of the field and the copse beyond.

"What did he die from?"

David put on the kettle for coffee before he sat down. "Let's eat." He hastily made himself a sandwich and stuffed it into his mouth.

"But…" Edda gave up. It was obvious whatever he was hiding he wasn't going to tell her anytime soon. She held up her hands in surrender and put together a sandwich for herself. "Another time."

Chapter Eight

Edda left David's house an hour later, none the wiser about his brother. She didn't want to pry so she'd decided to let David tell it in his own time. But David was not forthcoming.

She found her cell and called Lesley before she forgot.

"Lesley? Hi, it's Edda."

"Hey, Edda. How's it going? Are you ready to come home?"

"Well, in fact, I was thinking of extending the stay. That is, if you want to. I don't want you to feel obliged."

"Actually, it would help me a lot. The job is going great and it looks like they want to extend my current contract. How long do you want?"

"How about another two months? Is that okay with you?"

"Two mo— Err, sure. That's great."

"You don't sound so sure." Edda had a sinking feeling that her stay would be cut short.

"No, no, no. It would help me a lot. What's going on with you?"

"I feel relaxed here. I'd like to feel that a little while longer before I have to jump back into real life."

"Sure. Take as long as you need."

"Thanks, Lesley."

They continued exchanging pleasantries for a few minutes before ending the conversation. Edda tapped her cell against her chin. She had another two months.

On the dining room table was the envelope from Tamara, marked in big black letters with Confidential. Putting confidential on it seemed silly as it would only make the nosy even nosier. Edda put her finger under the gummed seal and tore it open. She peeked inside and emptied the contents on the table. There were a number of photos of two models in the same two dresses. This, of course, was what her bags were to complement. Among the other items was a DVD disc and a note from Tamara:

Edda honey,

Daniel begged me to ask you. I tried telling him you weren't up to it. His show is in three months and he wanted two of your "specials," as he called them. Edda, don't feel you're obligated to do this. Take all the time you need.

Tamara

It was short and sweet, as her letters always were, but she noted that Tamara had also sent along swatches of Daniel's material. Edda sat down and looked at the photos. Daniel was a special customer. Her first break came in one of his shows, and she had supplied a number of her "specials" for his various fashion outings after that. How could she deny him? But was she up to it?

There was no immediate spark when she looked at the designs. Maybe she wasn't ready. Edda went upstairs, found her laptop in the bedroom, carried it downstairs and waited patiently while it booted up. The DVD itself had no markings on it, so Daniel didn't want anyone to know what was on it. But she knew it would contain something magical that sprang from his fertile mind.

The video began and she leaned back in the chair. The two models from the photos paraded on a make-believe walkway, turning one way then the other to show her the various angles of the dresses, the light and shadow and how they flowed. These were as important as the material itself. She picked up the swatches and studied them, feeling their flexibility, texture, and warmth.

Despite her reluctance, she had everything she needed to complete the project if she decided to go ahead. Then Delia's words sprang to mind. 'Life goes on whether you decide to stop or not.' That was an epiphany. Her world had stopped and she thought the rest of humanity would mourn with her. When that didn't happen she suddenly felt insignificant in the grand scheme of things.

Edda ejected the disc and shut down her computer. She would sleep on it.

†

Even though it had only been a few days since her surgery the pain in her nose still bothered her and had the annoying habit of waking her during the night. This night was no different. She took the opportunity to relieve herself before she popped a pill. Facing the mirror, she looked at the image projected there. The two black eyes had started to turn green. Well, at least she didn't look like a panda anymore.

Her gaze fell on the view out the window. Try as she might she couldn't ignore the pull to look out at the cemetery. She shook her head. "Come on, Edda. Nothing to see here. Move along." Before she could even process the words she had just uttered, she moved the few steps to place her in front of the window. "Pathetic," she muttered to herself.

"I knew it!" she crowed. A light shone from the copse, this time ending in a shooting star flying up into the night sky. A skyrocket perhaps? Or was it something more ethereal? While she couldn't deny that the things happening around her were more than suspicious, did she believe they were of a supernatural nature? She didn't normally believe in such things. Then again, she normally wasn't jinxed like she had been either.

Edda contemplated her next step. She could talk to David about it, but she suspected that talking about this particular topic had reached its limit. Maybe it was a matter of how she picked her words.

She stood at the window a while longer. When it seemed that whatever was happening on that little hill had finished she switched out the light and crawled back into bed. The pill she had popped had finally kicked in and she felt herself slip easily back to sleep.

†

Edda did, indeed, sleep on it but was no closer to a decision about Daniel's request when she woke. She dressed and went for a walk in the hope of clearing her head. When she reached the small pathway that led to the cemetery, she found herself retracing the steps she had taken a couple of days before. The air was fresh and clean and the sun shone through the gathering clouds. For some reason she had an urge to take another look around. She wouldn't have long to investigate before the rain moved in. Out of breath, she finally arrived on top of the rise.

The cemetery was exactly as she had left it. "No, I'm sure I saw something," she muttered. She couldn't be wrong twice.

There was a thick scattering of leaves on the ground which, while not strange in itself, seemed odd. She looked up at the ring of trees. They didn't seem devoid of leaves. She walked past the headstones and studied the ground. Her gaze went from the trees to the cemetery. There were a few fallen leaves under the branches but the leaf cover seemed heavier over the open ground.

She moved over to the nearest headstone and kicked away the leafy blanket. The soil was undisturbed. Why would someone scatter leaves over a sleepy cemetery? "Damned kids." She rested her hand on the headstone and studied a patch of red ground into the stone surface. It appeared to be a waxy residue. She leaned down and scratched at the patchy red specks ground into the stone, which had left a red trail down the side of the stone and onto the ground. The streak of red disappeared under the covering of leaves. Whoever had used the candle had been there for quite a while.

Edda flicked away the leafy covering to follow the trail of wax. Her hand ran over the grass. She wasn't sure if she was expecting nature to talk to her, but she continued to stroke the grass as she thought. Her forefinger caught on an edge and the grass patch flipped up. Someone had carefully peeled back the grass to get to the grave underneath.

Edda looked up at the headstone. Here lies Josiah Miller. 1897 to 1953. May he rest in peace.

The rising wind picked up the leaves at random, throwing them into the air to fall like patchwork rain. There was a snap of a twig behind her. Edda looked around nervously. "Hello? Anyone there?"

The faint howl of the wind set her nerves on edge. *Eeeedddddiiiieeeeeee.* The howl spoke her name.

"Who's there?" Edda swung around in a quick circle to try and find the source of the sound. Only one person called her Eedie. "No, it can't be. June?"

The temperature dropped as clouds covered the sun. Edda felt the goose bumps on her skin, but she wasn't sure whether it was from the cold or the name.

"June, if it's you, give me a sign." Edda held her breath and waited for something to happen. Did she really believe in the hereafter? Did she want to? She'd had enough heartache already, so did she want more by knowing that June was close but out of reach?

"Get that thought out of your head right now!" Edda berated herself. Of course, she would.

Edda moved under the nearest tree and watched the approaching storm. Something brushed her arm and she jumped. "Geezus!" She moved to the other side of the tree to get a better view of her attacker. As far as she could tell she was alone, but was she? How long could she wait before the rain drove her inside?

"Cut it out, kids, or I'll tell your parents!" It was a hollow threat because she wouldn't know who the kids were even if she saw them. A stone came out of nowhere and hit her in the leg. "This is not funny!" she yelled.

Suddenly she wished David was with her, not that he would have been much help. He had already admitted he hated cemeteries, ghosts, and vampires. She knew she'd be holding his hand, but at least she'd have company.

There was a hoot of an owl, which seemed strange in the light of day. Edda peeked around the tree trunk toward the garden of gravestones and the trees that framed it. Her gaze skittered from one spot to another, hoping to catch a glimpse of whoever was trying to scare the life out of her. Something thumped down on her shoulder and she almost peed her pants.

"Storm's comin'."

The hand on her shoulder belonged to a man who she would have guessed at being anywhere from forty-five to sixty years old. He was scruffily dressed in jeans and a well-worn sweater. His feet were encased in worn work boots.

"I can see that. I don't know if I'd make it home."

"Not nice round 'ere during a storm," he stated as if fact. "Probably got 'nuther ten minutes, if'n you hurry…"

Edda got the distinct impression that he was trying to get rid of her. "Did you throw stones at me?"

"Heavens no, missus! We don't get many visitors here. They probably don't want you around."

"They?" Edda was nearly afraid to ask. "Who are 'they'?"

He nodded his head toward the cemetery. "Them. They like it quiet 'ere."

"I'm sure they do."

"Ghosts of the past are comin' back to claim their own."

"Ghosts of the past?"

"Long time ago. They left. Now they're back."

"Who are 'they'?"

"Too dangerous 'ere. Best leave 'em alone."

"I saw some lights out here one night last week. Do you know anything about it?"

"Probably 'em. They don't sleep. Probably they're now watchin' us." He looked around warily. "Best you leave, missus."

Edda had plenty of questions to ask but decided it was time to leave the nutcase standing next to her to his graves and trees, at least for now. She looked up at the darkening sky and made the decision to try and get home before the rain. "Well, goodbye then."

She took off down the gentle slope at a brisk walk. It would test her stamina to keep up the pace but she wanted to put as much space between her and the loony old man on the rise. She stole one last glance at the hill when she reached the street and saw him still standing there watching her.

Unfortunately, she missed her target by twenty feet, which was enough space for her to get drenched by the downpour. Her key jammed in the door and she stood on the stoop cursing. The key finally turned and she stepped inside, dripping onto the carpet.

Edda didn't stop. She continued into the kitchen to strip off her wet clothes. At least there she could mop up afterward. Her nerves were already frayed, but the stubborn resistance of the soaked cloth was her undoing. She cursed long and hard, and once she finally got out of her clothes she threw them into the laundry basin to worry about later.

Grumpily, she walked upstairs and into the bathroom to finally remove her underwear. Even a nice dry towel couldn't ease her frustration. She looked at herself in the mirror. "Why me?" she growled. When no answer came she left, padding across the hall to the bedroom to find dry clothes.

†

The rain finally stopped late in the afternoon. Edda took the opportunity to sit in the backyard and read.

"Well, hello stranger!"

Edda looked up from her book. David's head popped up above the fence. "Hello, David. How was your day at work?"

"Eh." She assumed he had shrugged his shoulders because his head moved.

"That good, huh?"

"More to the point, how are you? Did you survive without me?" He gave her a dazzling smile.

"I managed." Edda rested the open book on her chest.

"No demons or ghosts?" he asked jokingly.

"As a matter of fact…" The smile on David's face dropped. "I saw the light again last night. This time it flew up into the sky and hovered there for a few seconds."

"Uh-huh."

Edda knew that tone. He was humoring her. "No, really. I went out there this morning and some old guy jumped out of the bushes and told me about 'them' returning. Scared the life out of me."

"Them? Who are 'them'?"

"I don't know. I didn't stay around long enough to quiz him. I got the impression he was talking about the spirits in the cemetery."

"Sounds crazy to me."

"Maybe."

"So what are you going to do?"

"What can I do?"

"I dunno. You're the one with the fixation." Edda held him in place with a glare. "Okay, interest. Too many questions and not enough answers."

"Darn tootin' as my mama used to say." Edda stared vacantly at the fence. "Maybe I could check it out and see where the cemetery used to be. That'd be a good project for this week."

"Don't you have other things to do like, say, try getting back to work or something? What about the stuff Karen delivered?"

"I'm still thinking about that."

"It sounds like it's important."

"I know that!" she snapped. "Sorry, this nose is being a real pain in the a… You know what I mean."

"Posterior. Sure, I know what you mean. Keeping you up?"

"I hate taking those painkillers, but it seems to be the only way I can get some sleep." She sighed and let her head rest against the cushion. "How would I go about finding, say, the blueprints of the cemetery?"

"Plans for the cemetery? Hmmm…" His finger tapped his lips as he thought. "You could try the local Council Planning Department, but I don't know the address. Maybe you could check on the Internet."

"I don't have Internet access."

He looked at her astonished. "I thought everyone had Internet. Except the Amish. Are you one of them?"

"You know damned well I'm not." Edda couldn't stay mad at him for long. David always seemed to have a snappy comeback every time things got unsettled between them. She wondered what it would take to make him really upset.

"I'll look it up after dinner and I'll put a printout of the directions in your letter box when I leave for work in the morning."

She couldn't ask for more than that. "Thanks, David." She gave him her most charming smile.

"Do you want company for dinner?" He looked at her hopefully. What could she say?

"Sure. My place. Give me an hour."

"I'll see if I can find a bottle of wine or something. Of course, you could end up with Pepto-Bismol."

"Just for that, you're on dish duty tonight."

He laughed and walked away. Edda heard the back door open and close, leaving her to quickly think of something for dinner.

Chapter Nine

The next morning Edda went to the mailbox in expectation. Sure enough, there was a sheet of paper inside with a hastily scrawled message from David. *Happy hunting!* it said. However, the map only covered the immediate area around the building, not how to get there in the first place. Still, Edda remained confident that she could find her way into the city. After all, how hard could it be?

She cursed herself for not being more prepared. Follow the crowd had been her motto because she thought everyone was driving to work. After two detours to suburbs she'd never even heard of left her dazed and confused, she pulled into a gas station to ask for directions. Five embarrassing minutes later she was on the freeway to downtown.

Suddenly streets mentioned on the map began to appear and she felt more confident about finding the council building. When she turned onto the final street she muttered, "Hallelujah!" The large gray building loomed up from the sidewalk like some evil bureaucratic monolith. It looked daunting, and Edda suspected she would be spending some time trying to find the planning department. But first things first. She needed to find a parking spot.

Edda worked her way outward from the council building, going around and around the block without success. Her only option was to find a parking garage. On her next pass of the nearby streets, she spotted a small open patch of land that held a number of cars. One emerged and she drove in. "Any chance of a parking spot?"

The young man working there smiled at her and nodded. "Another five minutes and it would have been gone. I'll park it for you."

"Right place and right time, huh?" She grinned at him and climbed out of the car. He handed over a parking stub and she watched as he parked her beloved car. There was something about another person driving it that made her nervous.

The young man came back to his booth and hung her key on a vacant hook. "Anything else?"

Edda snapped out of her reflection. "Err, yes. Which way is the council building?" She had lost her bearings from the constant circling of the area.

He pointed to her right. "That way. First intersection, go right and two blocks down."

"Thanks." Edda set off at a slower-than-normal pace. Despite being discharged from hospital not long ago, she didn't want her stamina to flag before she'd even started. Luckily, the sun was out and the temperature warm. It seemed God was shining down on her this day. Now, she only hoped her luck extended to finding the information she was after.

As the man had said, the council building was two blocks down on the right of the intersection. If it were possible, it looked even more imposing up close. She readied herself for battle and walked inside. The large foyer had a constant influx of people passing through it. She approached the large reception desk sitting against the far wall.

"May I help you?"

"Yes, I was looking for the Planning Department."

The receptionist looked at Edda curiously. "You have an appointment?"

"I didn't know I needed one."

"If you're here to discuss a current project you will need an appointment."

"I wanted to look at plans for a project about ten years ago."

"You'll want the records department located in the basement."

"How do I get to the basement?"

The woman pointed to the elevators.

"Thank you." Edda nodded. The receptionist acknowledged her briefly before turning her attention to the next inquiry.

Edda wandered over to the bank of elevators and pushed the down button. Several moments later there was a ding and the opening of doors. She stepped inside and pressed B. She felt her stomach drop, but she wasn't sure whether it was the elevator or her nerves. What if they wouldn't let her see the plans? Was it so important that she did?

Another ding announced her arrival at the basement. She stepped out to face a short corridor. At the end were large glass doors. Emblazoned on one of them was Planning Records. Suddenly Edda felt like she was in a police station about to be arrested. She didn't know why she felt this way, but the sight of the two large doors intimidated her.

Gathering up what courage she had left, Edda walked the short distance to the office and pushed open the door. It was so quiet she knew she would hear a pin drop. On the counter sat a small bell, and without hesitation she rang it.

About a minute later a tall, thin young man walked up to the counter. "Can I help you?" He gazed over his black-rimmed glasses at her, giving her the impression that he was judging her, and she decided he probably was.

"I was wondering if I could look at the plans for Evergreen Gardens Estate over in Cambridge, please." Edda showed her best manners.

"All current applications…"

"…need an appointment, I know. I was after the original plans at the time of construction, about ten years ago. Specifically, I was looking for the location of the nearby cemetery."

"Are you a resident of this city?"

"I'm just visiting."

"Only residents can request to see council plans."

"I don't want to buy it. I just want to see—"

"Only residents can request to see council plans."

"So you said, but—"

"Only residents—"

"All right!" Edda rubbed one hand over her brow. "Is there any way I can make a special request to see the plans?"

He walked away and returned with a two-page form. "Fill this out and return it to me. A decision will take two to three weeks."

"Two to three weeks! I'm asking to see a bit of paper not steal the Shroud of Turin."

He looked at her with disinterest, the paper still in his hand. Edda snatched it away and said, "I'll be back." She left the office and stomped down the hallway to the elevator. She pounded the button and grumbled under her breath, "Damned bureaucratic red tape."

Edda stood on the sidewalk. "Well, that didn't go well." She spotted a woman walking toward her. "Delia! Hey!"

Delia slowed her walk and looked warily at Edda. "Hello."

Edda could feel the freeze from where she was. "How are you? I haven't heard from you in a while."

"I've been busy." Delia wouldn't look her in the eye.

"Look, I think there's been a mix-up," Edda responded quickly. "Can we at least talk about it over a coffee?"

Delia nodded and Edda led the way to a small coffee shop a hundred yards up the street. Edda waited for the coffee and tea to be delivered before she continued. "I assume the reason for your withdrawal has to do with the last time I saw you."

"It was."

"Karen pointed out my error. I didn't realize I had offended you." Edda waited for a reply but received none. "I wasn't pushing you away."

"It sure seemed like it to me."

"So Karen was right. It wasn't you, Delia, it was me. I was scared about people thinking that I would take up with another woman so soon after June's death. I wasn't thinking. Can you forgive me?"

Delia nodded but Edda felt it was a half-hearted admission.

"Heck, I don't even know if you are inclined that way." Edda inwardly cringed at her own words. Subtlety seemed to be lacking in her of late.

"I can't say I've thought about it."

"Thought about…surely you have…" Edda snapped her mouth shut.

Delia grabbed the sugar packets and opened two of them, pouring them into her tea. She stirred slowly and deliberately. "I'm on the wrong side of everything." She glanced at Edda and saw the confused expression. "I'm on the wrong side of a hundred and twenty pounds, the wrong side of forty and the wrong side of pretty. You get the picture."

Edda did indeed get the picture. Delia would be classified by her friends as a frumpy, middle-aged woman. While Edda couldn't fault the description, she knew there was a lot more to the woman seated across from her.

"What happened?"

"What makes you think something happened? Look at me!" Edda kept silent. "I took care of my sick and aging mother. By the time she passed on, so had my life. I trained for the only thing I was good at and that was looking after people. Here I am, approaching fifty and alone." Delia grabbed her cup and took a mouthful of her tea.

"You're not alone." Edda reached across the table, took her hand and squeezed it in comfort.

"Don't do that. You don't mean it."

"If I didn't mean it I wouldn't do it."

"Don't play games with me. I'm too old and too tired to fight."

"Damn it, woman!" Edda stopped and took a deep breath. "I'm trying to apologize."

"You've apologized. Your conscience is now clear." Delia drank the remainder of her tea and started to stand.

"Wait!"

"What do you want?"

"Can't we be friends?"

"Why? There's nothing to gain by it."

"You are a stubborn—"

"Go on!" Delia hissed. "Say it. Say it!" Edda closed her mouth. "I thought so."

Delia departed, leaving Edda with the check. She threw a few bills on the table and took off after her. "Slow down!"

"Leave me alone."

"And that's how it will be if you keep pushing everyone away." Delia stopped walking after hearing Edda's words. "That's it, isn't it? It's so you can wallow in your righteous self-pity. You have no friends, but you won't acknowledge that it's a situation of your own making."

"It's so easy for you," Delia said, "You have everything at your fingertips—looks, money, friends."

"But no partner," Edda said sadly. "I'm not pretty, my work is my mistress, and I'm alone."

Delia didn't reply for a few seconds. She sighed deeply and let her breath out slowly. "We're a right pair, aren't we?"

Edda blinked a few times in surprise. "I suppose we are."

"But you've got that pretty comment wrong."

"Oh, come on. Before it was broken my nose was crooked and my eyes are too far apart."

"If you say so, but at least people notice you."

Edda walked up to Delia and moved forward, hoping she would follow. "You are very striking, Delia."

"Oh, tosh."

"No, really. You have lovely eyes that reveal a lot about you."

"No, I don't."

"Yes, you do. You are compassionate, generous, and loving woman. You care about others and that's a rare trait these days." Delia blushed and Edda smiled. "Peace?"

"What are you doing here? I got the impression you stick close to home."

Edda noted the omission, but answered the question anyway. "I wanted to look at the plans for the estate but some head-up-his-ass pencil pusher wouldn't let me. He said something about me not being a resident."

"That sounds like my nephew Lucas. Come on."

"I'm so sorry—"

"What for? That's what he's like."

They walked back to the entrance of the council building and stepped inside. Edda let Delia lead the way even though she herself had taken the same route only half an hour before.

Delia opened the door to let Edda step through to the office.

"I told you—"

"Just wait until your mother hears about this!"

"Aunt Delia? What are you doing here?"

"Protecting a customer from you, or so it seems. Do you talk to everyone this way? No wonder you're still in the basement."

"Please! Not in front of a stranger!"

Delia had him shaking in his boots. "Your granddaddy would turn in his grave if he heard you talk to a woman like that!"

"Aunt Delia! Rules are rules." Edda tried not to laugh as Lucas valiantly tried to maintain his authority.

"I can vouch for her, Lucas. She's not going to steal your precious plans. Now, can you please get the plans for…where is it?"

"Evergreen Gardens Estate." Edda grabbed the paper and pencil sitting on the countertop and wrote down the address. "I believe the estate was built about ten years ago and I wanted to know what was there before it."

Lucas picked up the paper, looked at it and then stared at Edda.

"Well, chop-chop, lad." Delia flicked her fingers in a shooing motion. Lucas glared at her and left.

"I think the lad comment was a little over the top."

"I think you're right," Delia whispered. "Did you see the look he gave me?"

"Thank you for the help."

"Yes, well…it doesn't mean were bosom buddies or anything."

"You are going to make me work for this, aren't you?"

"Yup." Delia took a couple of steps away to study the plans mounted on the wall. "What's so important about the estate anyway?"

Edda smiled. If Delia expressed an interest there was a chance their friendship was still intact. "The night that I broke my nose? I'd been sick in the bathroom and I saw a light coming from the little cemetery in the field."

"What's that got to do with where you live?"

"That's what I'm trying to find out. David said the estate had been built about ten years ago. When I visited the cemetery it looked relatively new. The gravestones were old, going by the dates on them, but the stones themselves looked like they had been moved recently."

"Recently, as in the last year?"

"If my guess is right, recently as in ten years ago."

"So they moved the cemetery ten years ago. So what?"

"It may be nothing. It could be something. I don't know. It just bothers me, that's all. I've seen the light twice and the last time was a real doozy. It hovered for a while then shot straight up into the night sky and fizzled out."

"Fireworks?"

"Maybe. I don't know. I couldn't find any evidence of them. All I found was a smudge of wax on one of the headstones. Someone went to a lot of trouble to cover up whatever they were up to."

"A witches' coven."

"You have got to be joking!" Edda tilted her head back and laughed.

"Why not? Do you have another explanation for candle wax and a ball of light?"

"I suppose at this point it's as good a reason as any." Edda looked at her watch.

"Where is that boy?" Delia moved to the counter. "Lucas? What's taking so long?"

It was a few long seconds before Lucas returned empty-handed. "I can't find it. It's gone."

"And you were getting cranky about Edda losing it." Delia gave Lucas a stern look.

"It's not my fault!"

"I seem to recall you telling everyone last Christmas that you were in charge of the office. Are you saying that you lied?"

"Yes! No!! I don't know how it happened."

"You should have kept your mouth shut at Christmas."

"No, not that. Each plan is carefully numbered and recorded. If a council employee takes one they have to fill out a form. My records say the plans should be here, but they're not."

"So, someone has stolen them," Edda said.

"Looks like it. My ass is in the can."

"Or an employee has taken them without recording it."

"It's a possibility, but I've haven't seen anyone from upstairs for a couple of weeks now." Lucas moved to the wire tray filled with paper. He began to search through the pile. "If I found out who did this…"

"Come on." Edda pulled on Delia's arm and led her out of the building. "There's no point in hanging around. This will just have to remain a mystery."

"You could try the newspapers. One is four blocks from here in that direction." Delia pointed down the street past the coffee shop they had just been into. "They'd have back issues you could check. Or there's the library five blocks that way." Delia pointed in the opposite direction. "You could check with them concerning local history."

Edda smiled. "Thanks, Delia. You've been a great help. Let's go."

Delia stopped. "Sorry, you have to do this on your own. I'm taking an old patient grocery shopping this afternoon. Poor old dear can't get around much by herself any more." Delia's gaze dropped and she scuffed her feet in embarrassment. "Yeah, well, I'm a sucker for a sad story."

"Is that why you found me?" Edda asked.

"I…I don't know." Delia turned to leave. "Catch you later."

"Thanks!" Edda called after a rapidly departing Delia. As she watched, Delia looked nervously over her shoulder. Had Delia forgiven her? Only time would tell.

Chapter Ten

Edda started her walk to the newspaper office. In the next block she noticed a computer shop. She stopped and looked in through the window. Until now she had avoided using the Internet because she knew her email box would be full, and then some. For some reason, she felt maybe she was now ready to handle the rigors of answering all the questions she knew she would find concerning June's death. As David had pointed out last night, she was living in the land of the Amish and needed to move into the twenty-first century. She entered the shop and bought a USB wireless Internet service. Tucking her purchase in her bag Edda continued her journey.

Three blocks further on, Edda approached the glass doors of the newspaper office, barely noticeable against the wall of glass panels that ran the width and height of the building. While the council building had been all gray concrete, the newspaper building was an ultra-modern glass homage to modern architecture.

Once inside she found a large directory. There was a listing for Archives so she decided to start her search there.

What was it about records and basements? She found herself in another basement facing another bureaucratic employee. To her surprise, he was considerably more helpful than Lucas.

He directed her to one of the computer stations scattered around the large room and helped her to log on to the database. When he left she stared at the screen. Where to start? The most logical place was ten years ago.

†

Edda returned to her car three hours later with barely more knowledge than when she had arrived. The one positive she got out of the trip was how to access the newspaper's database. That would come in handy on her next trip to the city.

She reconsidered that thought. No, she had gained a number of positive things out of her little excursion. First and foremost, she had once again made contact with Delia and tried to sort out the confusion. While not a complete success, she felt some progress had been made in repairing that particular bridge. She now had the means to access the Internet and its search engines. Finally, there was someone else who had an interest in the estate and the cemetery. Maybe she wasn't going crazy after all.

Edda turned on the radio to try and drown out the little voices in her head, all expressing their own opinions on her sanity. She was too tired to fight it and just wanted to step back from all the questions she was trying to process.

She turned onto her street and knew she was seconds from home. David's car was conspicuously missing, but she expected that. He wasn't due home from work for at least another hour or so. She pulled up in the driveway and turned off the engine. A deep sigh of frustration escaped her lips.

Life had a way of butting into her grieving whether she wanted it to or not.

When she stepped inside the house she saw Tamara's envelope sitting on the cabinet, enticing her back to work. She couldn't put her decision off much longer. Daniel had been her best customer and he deserved her attention. Maybe it was what she needed to feel normal again.

Edda grabbed her cell and dialed Tamara's number.

"Tam?"

"Edda, darling. How are you?"

"Fine. I'm calling about Daniel—"

"It's not a problem, sweetie. I'm sure he can find someone else—"

"I was calling to say yes, in fact. I'll call you when it's ready for pickup."

"Really? Are you sure?"

"Tamara, I've never known you to turn down a commission. What's up?"

"Nothing, darling. Nothing at all. You just surprised me. When you left…"

"I was not in good shape. I know. There's only one way to get back on track and that's to climb back into the saddle."

Tamara chuckled. "You've never ridden a horse, Edda. When you decide to, give me a call."

"I asked for that, didn't I? How are things back at the office?" There was a moment's silence. "What's wrong?"

"Nothing."

"Tam!"

"The buzzards are circling, Edda. They think it's the end of your career."

Was it? Did she want it to be? She felt she still had a lot to give. All she needed was the motivation. "Not yet," she said with quiet determination.

"You go, girl!"

After she said goodbye and hung up, Edda found a mirror and stared into it. "Not yet," she muttered to herself. It was an affirmation more than a promise.

With the decision made, Edda went into the kitchen and made a cup of coffee. She returned and sat down with her coffee and the envelope, staring at it for several moments before opening the flap. She examined the contents again, this time with a critical eye. Somehow she would make this work.

Edda gathered her computer and booted it up. As it ran, she seriously considered using her new Internet access to do some snooping around. "Hold it, girl. Work first, then play." It took some steely resolve on her part not to give in to her newly honed curiosity.

A faint brush against her leg made her jump. She looked down to see feline eyes staring back at her.

"Decided to show up, huh? Traitor." Of late Jasper had taken to exploring his neighborhood. "Is David your new best friend?"

Jasper meowed. To Edda it sounded almost innocent. The cat, she decided, was just too damned smart for his own good. She picked him up and sat him on her lap, idly stroking him while she watched Daniel's presentation. It took another couple of repeat screenings before her mind latched on to what Daniel was looking for.

Edda picked up her pencil and started to sketch. By the time she had drawn something she could work with the light had faded to dusk. Jasper had long since dozed off in her lap and she could feel the ache of bad posture.

She gently nudged Jasper but he refused to move. Left with no choice, she stood with him in her arms and placed him on the sofa. "Spoiled cat," she whispered after she stood back and watched him stretch. Jasper's eyes opened briefly and gazed at her, before he curled his tail around his body and went back to sleep.

"Not hungry, huh? Your loss." She padded into the kitchen and opened the refrigerator to find something to eat. It was tempting to just nuke something from the freezer but she knew June would be disappointed. To her, the secret to life was eating responsibly. To Edda, any shortcut in the food area was a good thing.

Reluctantly, she took some vegetables out of the crisper and a piece of meat from the freezer. Unfortunately, she had no excuse to cut corners and resigned herself to cooking a healthy meal. Maybe she could cheat on dessert.

†

The next morning Edda started out on her daily ritual of a walk around the neighboring streets. As part of her route she approached the border of the estate, marked by two short walls and a large plaque. Next to the wall sat a house she had seen a number of times now. It was older than those on the estate yet seemed to be part of the community. As she walked along the sidewalk a man in his mid-forties exited via the front door. He sat down on an old chair on the veranda and sipped his beverage from a mug. Edda slowed her walk and smiled at him. He nodded at her in acknowledgment.

"Good morning," she called out.

"Morning," he replied before taking another sip.

Edda stopped at the far corner of his property. "Excuse me." She moved back a few steps toward his front gate. "May I ask you a question?"

He eyed her for a moment before he answered. "What do you want to know?"

"Were you living here about the time the estate was built?"

"Yes. Why?"

"I was just wondering about the cemetery out in the field."

"Come in," he offered.

Edda opened the gate and walked up the path to the front veranda.

"Sit down." He nodded toward an old sofa against the front wall. Edda perched herself on the edge of the seat.

"Now, what's this about the cemetery?"

"I have the impression that it wasn't where it is now. Is that correct?"

"No, it was originally on the estate. Why?"

"Just interested. I visited it the other day and the gravestones looked like they hadn't been there long."

"They must've brushed them off when they moved 'em." The man took another sip of his drink but didn't make an effort to offer Edda one.

"Does the cemetery have a name?"

"It used to be part of Saint Barnabus church. Some kids burned the church down a while back. All that was left was them graves."

"So it doesn't have a name?"

"Someone called it the Beggars' Coppice. Don't know why. Maybe somethin' to do with the souls buried there—vagrants, bums, and no-namers. They all live there."

"I know that coppice means copse. That's the small grove of trees surrounding it."

"Well, learn somethin' new every day." His dull brown eyes studied her. "Why are you so interested in that clump of dirt?"

"No reason really. I saw a light out there in the middle of the night last week. It just got me wondering."

"Huh. I didn't see nothin'."

"It could be just my imagination."

"Could be." He sat there jiggling his knee as if waiting for Edda to leave. "Anything else you want to know?"

"Did anything unusual happen at the time the graves were moved?"

"Nope."

"Are you sure? I mean it would have been pretty busy with workers all over the place. Something could have easily happened without anyone knowing about it."

"I was the night watchman on the place, missus. If anyone was sneaking around I would have seen it."

"And you stayed?"

"They sold me the house cheap-like if I kept an eye on the estate. Couldn't say no to that."

"No, I suppose you couldn't." Edda felt she had worn out her welcome and stood. "Well, thank you for your time, errr…"

"Tom."

"Thank you, Tom. My name is Edda."

She extended her hand and he took it, shaking it briefly before letting it drop. As she walked down the path to the sidewalk, Edda could feel his gaze boring a hole into her back. She gave him one last look and a wave and walked briskly back to her house. She had decided that some people were just born ornery.

✝

After her shower, Edda took her mug of coffee and sat down in front of her computer. She knew she should be working on the bags but now that she had a name she just had to find out more about the cemetery or, more precisely, its place in the field. The computer hummed to life and seemed to take an eternity to boot up. It was abnormally sluggish which gave her time to get a refill on her coffee.

"I've really got to stop drinking this stuff," she muttered. Jasper appeared out of nowhere and sniffed around the laptop. "Don't you agree?" He meowed at her and pushed his way to sit between her and the screen. He flopped down and landed on the keyboard. The computer jumped from program to program, opening and closing as Jasper moved to make himself more comfortable. "Out of the way you stupid cat! I've got my designs on this thing. If you break it, so help me…" She didn't complete the sentence because it was a useless exercise. Jasper didn't know what he was doing. Now why didn't she believe that?

"Are you going to move any time soon?" Jasper's hazel eyes stared at her while he purred loudly. "Oh no, you're not getting around me that way. Now shoo!" She waved her hands at him but he was oblivious to her request. "How about some milk? Do you want milk, you lazy interloper?" Jasper's ears pricked up and he meowed loudly. Even before she made a move he shifted from the laptop and leapt off the table. Edda decided that he was the smartest cat in the world. He knew exactly what he had to do to get what he wanted. It was blackmail…or was that extortion? Either way, it was underhanded but highly effective.

The two hours she spent surfing the Internet was an exercise in aggravation. Most of the links on her searches led to nothing, but what general opinion she could find appeared to be that the cemetery had been moved because of the new estate being built. One reference made mention of Beggars' Coppice, but that was it. Frustrated with her lack of progress, Edda turned her attention to the construction of the estate. A handful of names were mentioned in one article regarding the absence of some workers that had raised questions at the time. It appeared their disappearance from the workplace had never been followed up, so she didn't know whether there was foul play or they just left without notice. However, she made a note of the names for future reference.

Edda was oblivious to the fading light outside as she continued on with her search. Finally, she gave up in disgust as her search list ended.

"That's..." She looked at her watch and sighed. "...four hours I won't get back." Was it really that important?

She shut down her computer and went to the kitchen to rustle up some dinner. Before Jasper had the chance to annoy her, Edda filled his bowl with a tin of...something. There was a cat on the label and that was good enough for her. This gave her the chance to make her own dinner undisturbed.

After dinner Edda slumped on the sofa, resigning herself to watching mindless drivel on the television. She couldn't stop the questions from filling her mind. Would the light make an appearance tonight? Would she ever find out what it was? One sure way would be to see it but she could only do that by staking out the cemetery. She could hear David saying 'that would be foolish' and, if she was honest with herself, he'd be right, but she was sick of not knowing. Once and for all she would know what the secret was that was occupying her curiosity.

†

From her spot in amongst the trees Edda questioned the cleverness of her plan. It was now fully dark but that was only the halfway mark. From what she had seen, the light didn't appear until well after midnight. If it wasn't for her stubborn curiosity she'd be lounging on the sofa watching TV or, if she felt more energetic, trying to work on the bags. Tonight stubbornness won out.

It had taken a thorough search of the copse to find a suitable hiding place. Most of the tree trunks were too thin and her presence would be immediately noticed. The handful of trees with trunks sufficiently wide enough to hide her, were too far away for her to be able to hear what was going on. Then again, this adventure was not worth the effort of climbing into the trees.

As the night fell so did the temperature. Edda pulled her coat around her and nestled in against the tree trunk she decided was her home for the next few hours. She reached in her pocket and pulled out an apple, munching on it quietly as the sounds of suburbia receded into the night.

The air was damp and she felt the cold seeping up through the ground. Why couldn't she just accept David's explanation it was a mystery not to be solved? She could have easily wiped her hands of the whole mess and not feel guilty. But what if he was wrong? And that's why she was leaning against a tree on a long, cold, lonely vigil.

The frogs and crickets began their nightly song and Edda closed her eyes to listen. There was something soothing about the cool of the evening and the sounds of the nocturnal creatures, and she was glad she could take the time to slow down and absorb the peace of nature. Edda opened her eyes and looked up. The sky was full of stars. The estate sat on the edge of suburbia so the stars were not hampered by the city lights. It was beautiful and serene, and it was something that June would've appreciated.

June. Edda turned her thoughts to her partner. Was she looking down on her right now? What would she think of Edda's rash actions? Edda realized she had answered her own question. Rash. She hadn't given it much thought or planning. So was she already dismissing the stakeout as frivolous? If David were with her he'd be scolding her for taking such a risk. Not that he'd be there in the first place.

She hadn't given a second thought to not asking her neighbor on her night's escapade. Firstly, he had been at work all day and would be tired. Who was she kidding? She didn't want him along to be a bug bear about cemeteries and people rising from the dead, let alone his opinion of her vigil.

Edda let her mind wander for a while as the darkness took hold. She activated her cell and saw that it was only nine o'clock. Time was playing a waiting game with her…and she was losing. Without thinking she closed her eyes for a while.

†

Edda heard a murmuring of voices and opened her eyes. She hadn't realized she had dozed off but knew she must have. There was a faint glow emanating from the direction of the graves and a conversation taking place that she couldn't quite make out. Her mobile phone showed it was eleven. It was still too early by her reckoning, but she had to see who it was anyway.

She got to her feet and crept toward the sound. Luckily, the leaves underfoot were damp and pliant and made only a faint sound as she walked. The voices became louder and the conversation became clearer.

"Josh, please! I don't want to."

"What was the point of coming out here then?"

Edda could hear the anger in the boy's voice. She secretly supported the young girl and hoped she stood her ground.

"I thought you wanted to talk."

"I wanted to make out. We could have talked back in your room."

"Don't you love me?"

"Yeah…sure."

Like hell you do, Edda thought. Boys that age only wanted one thing.

"Couldn't we just lie back and look at the stars?"

Edda caught a glimpse of a sly smile on Josh's face. *Don't*, Edda silently pleaded.

"Yeah, we can do that."

Edda retraced her steps back to her hiding place and lowered herself to the ground. Was this the cause of her nocturnal sightings? It was going to be a long night.

The conversation waxed and waned, the girl's voice rising whenever Josh made a move on her. Finally, she must have had enough when suddenly the two kids stood up and left the copse.

Edda watched them leave, the boy stomping off in front of the girl. She wondered whether he was going to leave her to the darkness and just when she thought she'd have to intervene, he stopped and waited for the girl to catch up.

The darkness closed in around her as the light from their lantern disappeared. It was cold, dark and damp, and still only just after midnight. She'd give it one more hour then she'd quit.

The time crawled by and she felt herself checking her cell every five minutes. When the time finally hit one o'clock, Edda conceded defeat and trudged home. As much as she hated to admit it, this was one mystery that seemed destined to be unsolved.

The walk had woken her up and she continued on to the kitchen in search of her fix. She was tempted to resort to instant when the coffeemaker took its time coming to the boil, but she knew the fake stuff was not the same. Her body would know the difference and insist on the real thing. Who was she to argue with her body's demands?

Her coffee fix finally sated, Edda dragged her tired body up the stairs and fell gracelessly into bed. She was tempted to go to the bathroom window for one last look, but decided against it. "Screw it," she muttered and rolled over to sleep, not even bothering to change into her pajamas.

Chapter Eleven

morning coffee. The local newspaper had been helpful with her research so she felt a desire to reciprocate with her support. A few days after beginning this new ritual she moved past the national news on the website's main page to the local news and a small article on a John Doe being found under a bridge attracted her attention. The description was sketchy but sounded vaguely familiar. It took her a moment or two to make the connection. Was it the crazy old man who had confronted her at the cemetery? Someone needed to know.

Before she could even think about the ramifications of getting involved with the police, Edda found herself standing in front of the police station. It was the right thing to do, but that didn't remove the butterflies in her stomach. She always felt uneasy dealing with the law, even when it didn't involve herself.

Taking a deep breath she climbed the stairs and opened the front door. The foyer was busy with visitors and police coming and going. She stepped up to the desk.

"Good morning, ma'am. What can I do for you?"

She opened her mouth but no sound came. Edda cleared her throat and tried again. "I saw a report on the news this morning about a John Doe."

"Do you know him?"

"Not personally, but I think I can help."

The desk sergeant picked up the phone and called for a detective. "Take a seat."

Edda looked at the seats against the wall. Her choice was either the empty chair between two suspect people, a woman who looked like she was high and a derelict, or the wall. She was tempted to stand but when the derelict moved she took the empty seat. She glanced sideways at the woman who looked straight at her nervously. "Hello," she said quietly. The woman continued to glare at her before backing away. Whatever the woman had taken had her fidgety and hyper-vigilant, making Edda wish she was anywhere but where she was.

Edda stood and was about to make her escape when a man in his mid-forties approached her. "Ma'am, are you the one who knows the John Doe?"

"The name's Edda Case. I don't know him personally, but I may have seen him recently. I'm not really sure it's the person you have."

"I'm Detective Steve Webber. Come with me." He extended his arm in invitation and she reluctantly walked in the direction he pointed. He fell in beside her and opened the door at the far end of the corridor. "My desk is over here." He led the way and placed his hands on the back of the chair he wanted her to sit in.

"I don't have to look at a dead body or anything, do I?" She'd never seen a dead body in the flesh, so to speak, so she was a little nervous.

"We've got some pictures, if you're up to looking at them." He waited for Edda to sit before he settled his bulky torso in his own chair. "How do you know him?"

"I only met him once, last Tuesday at about ten in the morning. He was at the cemetery near Evergreen Gardens Estate."

"That's out in Cambridge, right?"

"That's the one. It's a fairly new estate. Been there about ten years. I believe the cemetery used to be there and it was moved to accommodate the estate."

"You seem to know a bit about it." His pen scribbled across the notebook on his desk.

"I did a little bit of research. There's been some sort of light at the cemetery in the middle of the night. Quite a mystery. I wondered if the cemetery had anything to do with the estate."

"And why do you think that?"

"I had an accident and was hit in the nose with a shovel lying on the ground. I didn't put it there."

"Hmmm."

"But that's not what I'm here for." Edda gripped her legs. "Can I see a picture of this man?"

Detective Webber opened a file and took out a photo. He slipped it across the table to her. The photo was of a dead John Doe. She studied the face intently. "I think it's him. I can't be a hundred percent sure. I only talked to him once."

"What did you talk about?"

"I went to the cemetery to see if I could find something to explain the light I'd seen the week before. He came out of nowhere and suggested I'd better leave before the storm broke."

"So he was trying to get rid of you?"

"He was rambling about 'them' not wanting visitors around."

"Them?"

"I assumed he was talking about the bodies in the coffins." Edda looked at the scruffy beard and the large head wound that had been discreetly hidden. "He did say something strange. Something about 'ghosts of the past coming back to reclaim what was theirs.'" Edda pushed the photo back across the table. "I assumed he was a caretaker or something of the cemetery."

"Anything else?" Webber was still writing as he asked the question.

"That's about it. I left after that. When I reached the street I looked back and he was watching me."

"What was your impression of him?"

"I thought he was a loony old man and probably homeless. His clothes were worn and had holes. He was unshaven and unkempt."

"That sounds like him." He looked up. "Can I have an address and phone number in case I have any further questions?" He pushed over a pad and pencil.

Edda picked up the pencil and began to write. "I'm house-sitting at the moment, but this is where you can find me."

"How long will you be staying?"

Edda stopped writing. "Another couple of months. If that changes I'll be in touch."

"Please do." He stood up and took her hand to shake it. "Thank you, Ms. Case, for coming in."

"I hope it was of some help."

"It's a place to start." He escorted her to the foyer. "Goodbye."

Edda was suddenly alone. She had done her duty. Now it was time to go home.

But home felt a little empty. The case appeared to be closed to her and now in the hands of the police. Why did that not fill her with confidence?

She knew David would be happy that it was done. Maybe she'd have a chance of things getting back to normal, or as normal as they were when she first arrived. Maybe she should think about expanding her circle of friends. That would be the sensible thing to do. She gave a fleeting thought to just returning to her apartment and picking up her old life. If she did that she knew she'd lose what she had with David and Delia. But what did she have?

David was a lot of fun, but their friendship had been rocky lately. And Delia? Well, Delia was an enigma. She wasn't quite sure what Delia was to her. A friend? A confidante? It seemed to be a gray area to her, and one she wasn't sure she should be poking around in.

Edda contemplated what she wanted out of her life and, in particular, the next year. It was probably too early to think about that, but she knew what move she could make that would determine whether she stayed or not…that is if Lesley agreed to it.

†

The next couple of days Edda applied herself to her day job, that of handbag designer. She managed to keep her focus and actually made progress on Daniel's specials. One bag she designed required some intricate leather weaving and she was engrossed in cutting strips off a piece of leather from her cardboard box full of tools and remnants. It had taken a few attempts to find the ideal width for braiding and she was currently in the process of trying various knots to achieve what she had in mind. This project was a little more elaborate than her usual bags, but the mental and physical

124

exercise in trying to create something more adventurous made her feel more like herself than she had in months. That was not to say that June wasn't too far away from her thoughts, but she was content that it wasn't her *only* thoughts. Maybe she could find her way past it all.

Edda put down her first attempt with the leather macramé and turned on the television for some background noise. The daylight was fading fast and she hadn't even noticed. She flicked on a light then picked up another pile of strips to begin again.

After a number of attempts she was still not satisfied with the lay of the leather. She was about to abandon the idea when she slapped her head. *D'uh!* Putting aside the leather Edda turned to her computer and did some research on knotting instead.

Finally, she found a page that was useful and she started to jot down notes. Jasper chose that moment to spring into her lap then onto the keyboard, sending the page fluttering off into cyberspace.

"What!" Edda had barely begun to accumulate the information she would need for her work. "Damn stupid…!" Before she knew it her hand was raised. What was she doing? She had never lifted a hand to him before and she wasn't about to start now. "Come on." She grabbed the cat off the keyboard and the staccato screen stopped. "Let's get some dinner." She glanced back at the computer and hoped she would be able to get back to the webpage. Absently she wondered if she could plait cat fur.

Edda sat at the table and watched Jasper devour his food. Tonight was a casual affair because she didn't want to waste time preparing food that would not be appreciated. She was in the zone, as June used to put it.

Jasper sat at her feet and meowed. A second later he launched himself at her and deftly landed in her lap.

"Oh, no, no, no. I have work to do." But Jasper refused to move with her gentle nudging. "Please, not tonight. At least, not now." She knew she was likely to look for his presence later in the night.

Edda lifted the cat. "You park yourself over here." She placed Jasper on the sofa, but he refused to let her leave and swatted at her hands. Every time she tried to back away to return to her computer he meowed at her until she returned and stroked him. "I haven't got all night for this." She grabbed one of the knotted leather samples and teased him with it until he was fully involved. Steadily she backed away and left him to his own devices.

Back at her desk, she eyed the screen with a certain amount of trepidation. As a safety precaution Edda rebooted her computer, hoping against hope that Jasper's ass hadn't destroyed her workbench. The cat growled and Edda smiled as she watched Jasper get wound up in the leather. He had created a prison for himself all on his own.

The computer hummed and clicked, so Edda took the time to untangle him. "Do that again and you lose your toy, buster!" She tried to sound stern but all she got for her trouble was a stare from those beguiling eyes. He knew exactly what he was doing. Whether she liked it or not, Jasper had found a new game and she was involved in it up to her neck. She had no one to blame but herself.

Surprisingly, finding the webpage turned out to be easy after she scanned her web history. "You just got lucky, pal," she muttered. While Jasper tired of his game and went to sleep, Edda continued on into the night.

It was one o'clock before Edda finally came out of her zone and realized it was late. She reviewed what she had learned and what she could do, and was well satisfied with her efforts. Jasper stirred as she stood up. "Time for bed." She shut down her computer, scooped him up and turned off the lights, slowly trudging up the stairs to bed. Dropping Jasper onto the bedcover, she dragged herself into the bathroom.

Edda looked at herself in the mirror. So much had happened to her of late. Was she really the same person who had started out on this journey? She doubted it. The daily influences on her life had changed dramatically, especially her newfound curiosity which had played more than a passing role in her life.

While brushing her teeth her gaze wandered until she ended up looking out the window to see if the small ball of light would make an appearance. As if on cue, the light appeared, taunting her like a red flag to a bull. She stopped brushing and stared. She had thought, mistakenly, that it would end with the death of the old man.

She rinsed her mouth and gave the cemetery one last look. "Don't do it, Edda," she whispered, because she knew no one would be happy with the announcement.

†

"Explain to me again why I'm doing this?"

"You want to find out the truth."

"No, that's not it because I know I don't care about the truth." David trudged behind Edda carrying two shovels.

"Fine. You're here to protect me from the dead rising up to get me."

"You just had to bring that up, didn't you? You couldn't have said I was here to make sure you didn't get into trouble."

"See? You do know. I don't have to explain anything." Edda smiled. "Careful, there's a small dip here." She heard David stumble in the pothole. Gingerly Edda led the way across the field toward the cemetery. While there was a full moon it was also necessary to use a flashlight to light their way.

"Do I have to mention again that it's against the law?"

"No. I got that the first ten times you said it."

"Why don't you just tell the police and let them dig it up?"

"I did and they did a cursory glance over the place today and left."

"Look." David stopped dead. "I didn't want to say this but…"

Edda stopped and turned to face him. "But…"

"You're becoming obsessive about this. Are you sure it's not because June is dead and you think this will bring her back?"

"Do you know how crazy that sounds?"

David remained silent. "So that's it, huh? You think I'm crazy." Edda stepped forward and snatched a shovel out of David's hand. "Fine. You can go home. I can manage by myself."

"Edda…"

"No. I don't need someone indulging my obsession. Thank you very much for your vote of confidence." She stomped away and continued her journey toward the cemetery.

"Edda!" David yelled. He trotted after her and called again softly. "Edda! Wait up!"

She stopped but didn't face him as he closed the distance between them.

"Why is this so important?"

Edda sighed. "I don't know, but it is. Maybe I need to see some proof that I did see that light. Maybe I need to know that I'm not going crazy."

"You're not going crazy."

"Can you say that for sure?"

"Let's get this over with." David walked past Edda.

"You didn't answer my question."

"You're not crazy, but I will be if we don't hurry up."

Edda followed David, shining the flashlight forward to help light his way.

"Grave robbing is a serious offense."

"I know."

"What if you find something?" David asked.

"I'll hand it over to the police."

"What if you find nothing?"

"We'll put the grave back the way it was."

"Will you visit me in the psych ward?"

"David, now you're being silly."

David stopped at the bottom of the small rise and allowed Edda to pass him. Reluctantly, he followed.

Edda shone the light at one gravestone, then another, until she found the grave she was looking for.

"Why this one?"

"It was the one that had the loose turf and candle wax."

"What loose turf?" Edda used her shovel to gently lift the grass up. "Oh, that loose turf." David placed his own shovel beside Edda's and they rolled the grass off the soil.

"This has been turned recently." Edda hunkered down and ran her hand over the surface. "It shouldn't take too long."

"If someone has already dug here what's the point of us digging?"

"You just want to get out of here."

"Damned straight!"

"Come on. We might find a clue." As to what the clue might be Edda had no idea, but if she didn't look she'd never find out.

"Why couldn't I just leave things alone?"

"What are you talking about?" Edda pushed the shovel into the dirt and pressed with her foot. As she suspected the shovel slid easily into the soil.

"Me and my stupid…" David muttered as he thrust the shovel viciously into the plot.

Edda stopped. "You and your stupid what?"

"Never mind." He lifted a large clump of dirt and threw it aside.

"No, I want to know. You and your stupid what?" Edda grabbed his arm.

David let go of the shovel and it stood firmly in the dirt. "Now you'll think I'm crazy."

"Then we'll both be crazy together. What's bothering you?"

David lifted his hands and rubbed his face briskly. "It's to do with my brother."

Edda said nothing and nodded.

"He…" David hesitated and drew in a deep breath, "…he committed suicide when he was seventeen."

Edda figured as much. It was something that David took to heart so she suspected there was some guilt attached to it.

"He was…gay. The teasing at school was intolerable. He couldn't take it any longer."

"How old were you?"

"Twelve. I saw he wasn't happy and I did nothing."

"David, it's not your fault," Edda said gently.

"I should have done something…anything. At least told my parents what was going on with him."

"Did you talk to him at all?"

"Yeah, but he said I didn't understand, that I couldn't know what he was going through. I told him I loved him anyway, but it wasn't enough. It was never enough." David dipped his head.

"And that's why you've been trying so hard to become my friend?"

"I don't want that to happen again. I'll be there for you, Edda."

Edda moved closer and pulled him into a hug. "I know you will," she whispered. Now it all made sense, and in a guilt-ridden way it was adorable. Edda rubbed his back gently while he composed himself. "Now, if you don't mind, I'm getting cold standing out here. Let's finish this and then you can tell me the whole story over coffee later." He pulled away from her and stared wide-eyed. "Oh no, you're not getting out of it. You got my story, now it's my turn to get yours." He nodded and moved back to his shovel.

By the time they hit the wood of the coffin they had both worked up a sweat.

"What now?" David asked uncertainly.

"Well, it seems a shame to have come this far and leave the coffin shut." She saw David shudder in the dim light from the flashlight.

"Do we have to?"

"You don't have to watch. Help me into the hole." Edda didn't want to be the one to do the deed but David seemed firmly set against it. She felt the cold rise as she was lowered into the grave. "Hand me the shovel." It took a great deal of effort to clear the soil away from around the top of the lid and it took nearly half an hour before she was satisfied with the result.

The light wavered as the flashlight shook in David's hand. She passed him the shovel and reached for the screwdriver in her back pocket. "Here goes," she muttered. Edda glanced up at her criminal companion and saw the terror in his eyes. She had to hand it to him, despite everything he was still there.

The screws were full of dirt and moisture and proved difficult to move. "Looks like whoever was here before hadn't gotten into the coffin."

"What makes you say that?" Edda could hear the fear in David's voice.

"These screws haven't been touched in years." She was about to scream blue murder when the first screw gave way. "Finally." Edda slipped the screw into her pocket. The remaining screws came away a little more easily, but not before a curse or two escaped her mouth. "Damn."

"What?"

"I've got no room to move to get the lid off."

She could hear his deep sigh from where she stood. He was going to do something he really didn't want to do. "Come here." He offered his hand to her and pulled hard, easily lifting her out of the hole. "So much for your plan."

"It's not my fault."

David opened his mouth as if he were about to say something but he stopped. "No, it's no one's fault."

Edda wondered if he was thinking of his brother when he made the comment. It seemed his guilt reared its ugly head once more.

David left Edda by the grave and went off in search of something. Edda watched the light zigzag across the expanse of grass, finally coming to rest on a fallen branch. He returned to her and handed her the flashlight. David stripped off some of the smaller branches until he had a manageable length of wood to pry off the lid. He lay down on the ground and dipped the branch into the grave. Edda joined him and shone the light into the hole.

"I just bet you were an Eagle Scout or something."

"Something like that." David's gaze met hers and he smiled. She patted his arm and allowed him to return his gaze to the hole.

It took numerous attempts to get the branch end to rest on the side of the coffin and even more attempts to get the branch to hook the far edge. David pulled firmly and steadily and the lid swung open like a door.

"Holy…!" David said.

"… shit!" Edda completed for him.

"Are you seeing what I'm seeing?"

"Sure am."

"What do we do now?" David asked.

"Like I said before, we contact the police. Do you have your cell with you?"

"In my back pocket."

"That won't be necessary."

The third voice came out of nowhere.

"Awwww."

Edda could smell the pee. David really did not like graveyards.

"Stand up." The voice moved closer and Edda saw that it was a policeman.

"But officer—"

"You are under arrest. Desecrating a grave like that, how could you?"

"But officer—"

"No excuses. There's a vehicle waiting back on the street. The two of you make your way—"

"BUT OFFICER—"

"What! You really are asking for trouble."

"Look in the damned hole!" Edda pointed at the hole in question.

"What can be so import…" The officer reached for his walkie-talkie and called for backup. He drew his gun and pointed it at them. "Trying to get rid of the evidence, huh?"

"No, of course not."

"Put your hands up!"

David's hands shot up into the air while Edda's made a more cautious reach. "Don't move!"

"You don't understand," Edda tried to say.

"Oh no, you don't understand. I've caught you red-handed. You're going to get a lengthy jail sentence for this."

"I'm the one who alerted the police in the first place."

"And that was a stupid move on your part."

"Officer!" Edda yelled. He stopped and blinked at her. "I talked to Detective…errr…Watson, Wilson…whatever his name was. I told him someone was snooping around here."

"A likely story."

"You can check it with him."

The policeman glanced over his shoulder at the sound of approaching footsteps. "It'll have to wait until morning. In the meantime we have a nice quiet cell waiting for you."

"Then I suggest you get someone to babysit this site in case the real perpetrator returns to finish his job." *Or my alibi disappears*, Edda silently added. Without the evidence in the coffin her goose would be cooked.

Edda remained silent as the two policemen cuffed them and escorted them to the parked car on the street. David and Edda were in the backseat of the patrol car when another patrol car pulled up. A few words passed between the policemen then the two arresting officers drove them to the police station. It was going to be a long and uncomfortable night. Would David ever forgive her?

Chapter Twelve

"I said we'd take care of this."

Edda opened her eyes and saw the detective on the other side of the bars.

"That was a really stupid thing to do," he said.

"I had to. You guys didn't believe me." Edda moved to sit on the edge of the bunk.

"We sent a patrol."

"Who waited five minutes then left. They didn't even look."

"The report said there was nothing to find."

"I saw them, Detective. They poked at the ground and left. It was a cursory look at best."

"That still doesn't give you permission to dig up a corpse."

"I understand that, but look what we found."

The detective grabbed the bars in both hands and sighed deeply. "And that's probably going to save you from a prison sentence." He nodded his head and the jailer opened the door. "Come on."

"What about David?"

"Get the other one and bring him to my desk," he told the jailer.

"Detective errr…I'm sorry, I've forgotten your name," Edda said.

"Webber, Steve Webber." He led her through the station to his desk. He pointed at the visitor's chair and plopped down into his own.

"Webber." *Well, I got the first letter right.* "Haven't you ever had a gut instinct about something and you just have to know whether you're right or not?"

"Yes, but the difference is that I'm the law, you're not."

"Look. I'm sorry I had to resort to such drastic measures, but look what we found."

"And what do you think you've found?"

"Haven't you seen it yet?" Edda was surprised he hadn't taken a look for himself.

"I went out there at first light."

"And?"

"And, what? This is no longer your concern."

David arrived and gave Edda a grumpy stare.

"It looks like you have more on your hands than just a mystery," Detective Webber said. "Why don't the two of you go home and let us do our job."

"But Detective Webber…Steve…please," Edda begged.

Steve glanced to one side and returned his gaze to Edda. "I can't discuss this with you. It's a police matter."

"I agree, but you must have some theory about that second body in the coffin."

"Maybe someone was trying to save money by burying the two together," David offered.

"No. The corpse on top was still decomposing," Edda explained. "The corpse on the bottom was a skeleton. They were buried at different times."

"So, do you have a theory on this, Miss Case?" Steve leaned on his desk.

"Edda, please." She gave him a smile in the hope of sweet-talking him into keeping her in the loop. "I thought about it last night. I think the corpse on the bottom is the original inhabitant. The second one may have been added when the cemetery was moved to the present location about ten years ago."

"How do you know that?"

"I asked around." Edda felt proud of herself. She knew something they didn't, at least for now.

"Its quiet location would allow anyone to bury the second body at any time," Steve countered.

"True. Can you test it to find out?"

"We can."

"What about dental records?"

"They're only of use if we have a name to put to the victim. We can't just go and look at every record one by one. We can only use it to confirm identity."

"Damn!"

"Unless we find a name we can't check it out." Detective Webber stood and extended his hand. "Now, if you'll excuse me, I have another murder to solve."

Edda stood and took his hand. "Thank you for getting us out of jail."

"You may not be so lucky next time. Promise me that you'll leave this to us."

"No more digging up graves. I promise." Edda mentally crossed her fingers. If he thought she'd drop it he had another thing coming. The discovery of the extra body in the coffin added fuel to her curiosity. "Come on, David, let's go home."

"But my shovels…"

"I'll buy you new ones." Edda pushed David toward the door. Once outside David shifted away from her. "What's wrong?"

"You know damned well what's wrong! I was in jail, Edda, all because of you and your stupid obsession. Why couldn't you just leave it alone?"

"But look what we found."

"Edda, here's some free advice. Leave the mystery to the professionals." David stomped off down the street leaving Edda standing outside the police station with her mouth agape.

"Okay." It seemed she was the only one who believed in her. If that was the way they wanted it, then she could easily work alone. "Oh, crap!" David had left her to find her own way home.

Edda only had one choice and that was to grab a taxi. It was going to be expensive but she had no cash on her until she got home. The meter ticked like a metronome and she knew each click meant money to her. If David hadn't been so angry she would have had a chance to share a cab with him and halve the bill. She wondered if David would ever forgive her.

When she finally reached home around midmorning, Edda's energy was about tapped out. She found her wallet and paid the cab before she dragged her tired body inside the house. The prison bunk did little to ensure her a good night's sleep and the adrenaline rush quickly faded. Edda trudged up the stairs to the bedroom. She slipped off her shoes and lay down.

Despite her exhaustion sleep didn't come easily. Her mind went over the previous night's adventure and it suddenly hit her that she had seen a dead body or, more to the fact, two dead bodies. Her stomach churned as the image of the macerated corpse lying on top of the skeleton appeared in her mind. "Nope. Not good." She barely made it to the bathroom before she threw up.

This was where it had all started—vomiting into the bowl. Edda glanced out the window without thought and saw two policemen standing guard over the crime scene. She could barely see the yellow strip of police tape used to cordon off the area. If it had been her in charge she would have removed the coffin, filled in the hole and hid the officers to see if someone would come to dig it up. Did that mean that Detective Webber didn't believe her story?

Maybe she wasn't cut out for amateur detective stuff. After all, what detective would throw up at the memory of a corpse? Still, she had felt the thrill of excitement when she uncovered the evidence, and it had left her wanting to find out more.

Gingerly, Edda returned to the bed and lay down. She tried to block out the images and concentrate on her obsession with the case. Was David right? What was driving her to pursue a matter that was best left to the police? She'd never been a nosy person before and had been content to let others solve the mystery, but this time the feeling of accomplishment and, dare she say, danger was a little intoxicating. Did she want to risk her life again for that thrill?

Edda had always thought herself content with her career, but at that moment she felt she needed something more. Had June's death pushed her to flirt with death herself? "Now you're being silly," she muttered.

There was a swift blur in her peripheral vision before she felt the impact of something hitting her side. Her heart rate soared and thumped heavily in her chest. Edda's hand shot out and touched the cat who had slumped down beside her. "God, cat. Don't do that!" Another wave of nausea hit her. "This is getting old." Edda rushed back to the bathroom and stayed there for another half hour.

†

Edda felt the solitude after four days. David had completely ignored her, even to the point of disappearing from his backyard whenever she stepped out the back door. He was really pissed at her. While she would have preferred his disappearance when she first arrived, his quirky need to see her all the time had grown on her. Edda missed him.

She used the time to work on her commission during the day. At night, however, her inquisitiveness brought her back to the Internet and the search for the truth. Surely the second corpse had to surface when the cemetery was moved. She therefore concluded that it was probably the most obvious time frame to search. With so many strangers moving around and digging the disposal of a body would be simple.

Edda focused her search on the estate, the cemetery, and the time frame. All of the reports basically said the same thing—the cemetery was moved to accommodate the new estate and the copse of trees in the nearby field seemed the best place for its relocation. She was about to give up on the project when she found a small article concerning the workmen on the estate project. Hidden amongst the one-column report was the mention of a handful of men disappearing from the site. The company had suggested that they had just left. But what if they hadn't?

She scrambled around in her notes to find the list of names she had jotted down earlier. Was one of them the victim or, worse, the killer? Every cell in her body was screaming to find out, but how? Where would she start? If she found out who it was, then what? She promised herself to hand over the information to Detective Webber, even though she knew she could do that now without risk to her, now that the body had been uncovered.

Edda didn't know what to think. Why did she need to solve this mystery? Ego? A need for completion? She couldn't discuss it with David, so that left her with one option.

Edda picked up her cell and dialed the number on the card tucked into her wallet.

"Hello?"

"Hi Delia, it's Edda." The silence from Delia wasn't promising. "Ah, I was wondering if you were free for dinner tomorrow night. Say seven thirty?"

"Errr…" Delia hesitated.

"I just want to talk, okay? Nothing funny."

"Why?"

"I just want someone to talk to. Is that all right?"

"I suppose so." But Delia's tone sounded anything but enthusiastic.

"If it's going to be too much trouble..."

"No! You just caught me off guard."

Edda was about to say why David was unavailable but she decided to keep her mouth shut. Delia's friendship was already on thin ice.

"Good. Seven thirty then."

"Where?"

"My place okay?"

"I…suppose…so," Delia repeated slowly.

"Or we can eat out if you want. You can pick the place."

"No, your place is fine. Do I need to bring anything?"

"I don't think so. I have to admit I haven't thought that far ahead yet."

"Seven thirty."

"See you then. Bye." Edda hung up and wondered if she had made a big mistake. Looking back over the conversation she realized how Delia could have taken her words. She had invited the woman to a dinner she had barely given any thought to. Maybe she should have gone with the dinner at a restaurant.

†

Edda's morning walk took her past David's house and she looked wistfully at it. His car was missing so she knew he would be on his way to work. She put in the earphones and switched on her music. Her ears buzzed with the sound of eighties rock as she walked. Her pace fell in time with the music as she covered her regular lazy loop of the estate.

She had taken this route many times and her daily constitutional ran like clockwork. She was a creature of habit and the walk wasn't something she wanted to break any time soon. The regularity of her routine was, for some reason, comforting. It made her feel somewhere near to normal— except that June wasn't there. It had been a painful path but Edda could feel herself coming to terms with June's death.

Wrapped up in the pounding music and her own thoughts Edda continued her walk, waving to the odd car that passed her. Her walk normally coincided with some of the moms taking their kids to school and she had come to recognize each car as it zipped by. It was another routine that had slowly dragged her into the little community.

As she approached her own street she glanced over her shoulder and saw one of the moms returning home from school. Edda turned her gaze to the sidewalk in front of her and kept up her steady pace. Breakfast was going to taste good this morning. This led her to think about what she would cook for Delia. As much as she hated the chore she felt it was necessary to show Delia she took the dinner seriously.

Edda looked over her shoulder once more, wondering what had happened to the car. It should have passed her, unless it had slowed down or stopped. Edda's eyes grew large. Careening down the sidewalk was the vehicle, weaving back and forth as the woman inside wrestled with the steering wheel.

Edda suddenly found herself in the path of the out-of-control car and she had to take action. She ran. The car followed her, inching closer with each step she took. Edda looked around frantically to find a safe way out. Finally, she dove over a low hedge into someone's front yard and rolled over. The car cut a clean path through the same hedge and moved toward her prone body. Edda's eyes widened as the grill filled her vision. Vainly she held up her arm to protect her face and closed her eyes.

A second passed…and then another. Edda opened her eyes and saw the front of the car mere inches from her face. The heat from the radiator rolled over her, escalating the temperature in her already warm body. Her chest hurt and she wondered if she was having a heart attack. It certainly felt like it.

The car's horn cut through the silence of the neighborhood and drew out those who were at home. The owner of the damaged hedge came out to find a car in her front yard.

"Oh Lord. Is anyone hurt?" She fussed around the car and finally realized that Edda was nearly underneath it. "Oh Lord!"

Hallelujah! Pass the collection plate! Edda silently added. She would have to say a silent prayer or two tonight. "I…I don't think so. Check the driver."

The woman did as she suggested and Edda slowly put her weight on her hands to remove herself from danger. Pain spiked through her left wrist and she pulled her hand away quickly. The pain subsided to a dull throb and she wondered what damage had been done. Tentatively she moved her hand. While the pain was present it was tolerable. Maybe she was lucky and hadn't broken anything.

"Call 911!"

The neighbors approached the scene and Edda found herself being pulled away from the car and out of danger.

"Are you all right, dearie?"

She looked up into the concerned face of an elderly lady.

"I think so. Thanks." She tried to stand but couldn't get any leverage with her injured wrist. Two women came forward and helped her off the ground. Edda tentatively tested out each limb. Besides a few niggling pains from bruises and scratches her wrist seemed to be the only damage to her body. But that didn't stop the EMTs from loading her into their van and taking her to the emergency room.

Chapter Thirteen

Hours later, the doorbell rang and Edda opened the door. "Oh Lord, what have you done?"

"It wasn't my fault!" She just knew Delia would blame her for it.

"Can I come in?" Delia slipped past Edda standing in the doorway. "Are you always this clumsy?"

Edda closed the door a little harder than she had intended. "Clumsy? I am not clumsy. This wasn't my fault."

"So you say. I brought this for dinner." Delia removed her coat and slung it over the back of a chair before handing Edda a bottle of wine. She plopped herself down on the sofa. "What happened?"

"The short version is I nearly got hit by a car."

"Good Lord! Was anyone hurt?"

"The woman in the car got a knock to the head and I sprained my wrist. The doctor said to keep it elevated for a couple of days." Edda jiggled the sling supporting her wrist. "It's okay. I must have jarred it when I dove over the hedge."

"You dove over a…hedge?" Delia's eyes widened. "I'm impressed."

"I didn't think I had a lot of choice in the matter. It was either that or end up as a smear on the sidewalk." Edda sat down in the chair opposite the sofa. Delia watched her and Edda found herself looking back at her. "I'm fine…really. I can't say the same for dinner."

"It's not a problem. Do you want me to go? We can always make it another time."

"Can you stay? I'd like the company."

"Do you want me to cook dinner?" Delia made a move to get up.

"How about takeout? There's a few magnets on the fridge with phone numbers for local restaurants." Edda leaned on her good elbow and pushed herself forward. Before she could stand Delia was by her side lending assistance. "Thanks." Edda could feel the warmth of Delia's supporting hand through her clothes.

"Maybe you should stay put." Delia's statement was more a gentle insistence. "I think you're still in shock. Here, give me the bottle."

Edda settled back in the chair and watched as Delia disappeared into the kitchen. She returned with a handful of fridge magnets.

"What do you feel like?"

"You're my guest. You choose. I haven't eaten since…" Edda was about to say breakfast, but then she remembered she hadn't had that either. "Hmmm, last night. I'll eat just about anything." She watched Delia juggle the magnets as she decided on dinner. "Thanks for coming over."

Delia looked at her sheepishly. "I'm sorry I haven't been sooner."

"Are you still angry with me?"

"A little." Delia turned her gaze to the magnet in her hand. "How about Italian?"

"That sounds great."

Delia reached into her bag and pulled out her cell. She dialed the number on the magnet and placed an order. Delia returned to the kitchen and reappeared a moment or two later with a glass of wine in each hand. She handed one to Edda.

"You thought I was playing some game with you," Edda said.

Delia ducked her head. "Something like that."

"I'm really sorry about that. As I said before I was trying to make the point that I wasn't looking to replace June so soon."

"It didn't sound like that to me."

"That's what Karen said. It's not what I meant."

"And how do you feel about that now?"

"Now? You mean about finding someone else?" Edda was taken by surprise. "Why?"

"No reason. Just making conversation."

Edda stared at Delia, trying to understand what she was not saying. "I didn't know you were interested."

"I'm not. As I said, just making conversation."

"I suppose I'll know when the time is right. It's only been three months."

"I wasn't suggesting that you do anything right now. I was just curious as to what you would consider a suitable time for grieving."

It was a strange question. "You've never…?"

"No, except when my mother passed, but that's not the same thing, is it?"

"No, it's not the same. I don't know if the ache will ever go away. But I'm glad I found a new friend." Edda smiled at Delia and received one in return.

Delia changed the subject. "Why did you come here?"

"Lesley offered this place to us when June was alive but she was too ill to travel. After the funeral there were so many calls, all offering help and wanting to talk about it. It was all too much."

"You could have just changed your cell."

"I suppose I could have. Settling the will was a nightmare."

"How so?"

"June's sister blamed me for everything…June's illness, June's death, her own plight…everything. She didn't think I deserved to be included in the will."

"Sounds like a bitter woman."

"Downright hateful, if you ask me. I had to get away from all the bickering. I found Lesley's letter and called. She needed a place to stay and the swap was beneficial for both of us. So here I am."

"How long are you staying?"

"I don't know. It was supposed to be two weeks, then four. Now it's up in the air. Lesley needs the apartment for at least six months so I suppose that's how long I'm staying."

"And your boss doesn't mind?"

"I'm my own boss, so the work gets done when I'm ready."

"It would be nice to have a job like that. Shift work is very wearing."

"And would play havoc with your love life," Edda said. Delia took a long swallow of her wine while Edda bit her lip.

"I don't socialize much."

"But surely you must have had time to find a boyfriend." Delia remained silent. "Girlfriend?" The silence extended for a few more moments. "Someone hurt you." Edda could see the sadness in Delia's eyes. "Besides me."

Delia nodded. "A lifetime ago."

"So you're letting life pass you by because of some jerk."

Delia's gaze rose to meet Edda's. "It's none of your business."

"True, but—"

"No! I don't want to discuss it." Delia looked around the room but not at Edda.

"So, why did you come?" Edda asked.

"You asked me to."

"You could have said no. It's not like we're joined at the hip or something."

"Why didn't you ask David?"

"Well…" Edda gulped loudly. "He's pissed off with me at the moment."

"That wouldn't surprise me."

"And what does that mean?" Edda glared at Delia.

"You seem to have a love–hate relationship with everyone you meet."

Edda was about to answer but then stopped herself. "We went to the cemetery and dug up a grave."

"You did what!" Delia shook her head. "You do know that's illegal."

"That's what David said a number of times."

"And you didn't listen?"

"I thought the police would understand. We discovered a second body in the coffin."

"The police would u—" Delia shook her head harder.

"What?"

"You, my dear girl, are an idiot."

"They wouldn't listen. What was I to do?"

"Forget about it?" Delia offered.

"But look what we found! It's an unsolved murder."

"Edda, it's not up to you to go around and dig up graves. It's illegal and highly unethical. No wonder David is angry with you."

"They didn't press any charges."

"That was probably because you did find something. If you hadn't they would have thrown the book at both you and David."

"He says I'm obsessed."

"Maybe he's right."

"Do you think I'm crazy?" Was she looking for absolution from someone?

"Crazy? No. Obsessed? Maybe. Why is it so important?"

"I don't know. I'm not sure what I think anymore."

"Maybe you're focusing your energy on this as a means of giving your life some order."

"Do you think so?"

"Then again, you could be just plain crazy. Cheers!" Delia lifted her glass and toasted Edda.

"I'm being serious here."

Delia sighed. "Look, the police have it in hand now. Why not just leave the crime solving to them?"

"Maybe because I'm not too impressed by how they've managed the case so far."

"Did they find out what caused the accident this morning?" Delia asked.

"That's the strange thing. The officer thought it looked like someone had cut up some barbed wire to make spikes and threw them on the road. Why would someone do that? What is the point?"

"Maybe someone was trying to kill you."

"Some…one," Edda immediately thought of Gail.

"I'm kidding, Edda."

"No, you may have a point."

"Now you're being paranoid."

"We'll see." Edda put down her glass on the table beside her chair and started to get up.

"Where do you think you're going?"

"I need to get my phone."

"Where is it?"

Edda thought for a moment. "In the kitchen near the knife block…I think."

Delia went into the kitchen and returned with both Edda's cell and the bottle of wine. She handed over the phone then topped up the glasses, leaving the bottle on the table next to Edda's glass.

Edda searched her memory for the phone number. She dialed and waited as it rang. "Hello? Sarah? It's Edda."

"How are you? We heard you'd left the city for a while."

"I'm fine, Sarah. I just needed a break. How's the family?"

"They're still coming to terms with everything. What can I do for you?"

"I was just wondering if Gail was around."

"You want to talk to Gail? I thought she'd be the last person you would want to talk to."

"I thought I saw her today, but I wasn't sure. I thought I'd check with you. Is she home?"

"As a matter of fact she left suddenly a few days ago. She muttered something about an emergency in Graham's family. Do you want me to get Gail to call you?"

"Heavens no!" Edda said almost harshly. "I thought I'd just check with you. I must have been mistaken. Thanks, Sarah, and take care."

"It's good to hear from you, Edda. Stay well."

"You too. Bye." Edda hung up and looked at the cell.

"Who's Sarah?"

"June's mother."

"And Gail?"

"She was the one I told you about. She's June's sister who would most like to see me dead. So your comment wasn't too far from the truth."

"I didn't mean it seriously. Come on. She'd have to be crazy to try something like that."

"Crazy. That seems to be the word of the day. Gail was pretty pissed, so I wouldn't put it past her to try something."

"Does she know where you are?"

Delia had a point. Edda had made sure that no one in June's family knew where she was. It would have to be blind chance that Gail had found her. "No, she doesn't."

"Then stop worrying."

"But what are the odds of the accident happening while I was on my walk?"

"Maybe it was just a coincidence that you were there when it happened."

"But it doesn't make sense—"

The doorbell rang and Delia answered it. She took a few bills from her purse and paid the delivery boy. "Dinner's up. Where do you want to eat?"

"The dining room table I think."

"No kitchen table?" Delia asked.

"Not tonight. We need something a bit classier."

"Well, sit down and I'll get the knives and forks." Delia helped Edda up and pushed her toward a waiting chair. While Delia fumbled around in the kitchen she brought the wineglasses to the table. She waited patiently until Delia returned with plates and cutlery. Delia had barely sat down when the doorbell rang again.

"Again?"

"Maybe he didn't like my tip." Delia grabbed her purse on the way to the door. "I'm sorry it's all I had," she said as she opened the door.

"May I come in?"

"Edda! It's David!"

"Come in! Come in!" Edda said excitedly.

David entered the living room, followed by Delia. "I just wanted to see if you were all right."

"It's nothing really. I believe it was—"

"An accident!" Delia interrupted. "The car blew a tire and the driver lost control. She happened to be in the wrong place at the wrong time." Edda looked at Delia as she spoke. "Isn't that right?"

"Yes, she's right," Edda said absently.

"As long as you're okay." David turned to leave.

"We were just about to eat. Come and join us."

David looked at Delia and then at Edda. He hesitated.

"Please, David," Edda said quietly.

Slowly, he moved around the table to sit opposite Edda. Delia went into the kitchen and returned with another plate, knife, fork, and glass. "Help yourself to the wine."

As Delia made herself comfortable David reached for the bottle. He filled his glass an inch or so before placing the bottle back on the table.

"How have you been?" Edda said quietly.

"Busy with work. You know."

"Yeah, I know." Edda poked at the food on her plate. "I haven't been near the cemetery since you left."

"That's good to hear." David handed his plate to Delia who spooned on a serving of the pasta.

"It hasn't stopped me from doing some research though."

David grabbed his glass and took a gulp of wine. Swallowing it he took a deep breath and asked, "Why can't you leave it alone?"

"David…" Edda reached out her hand to touch David's arm. "I'm not trying to get anyone in trouble. I just have to know the answer."

"And you can't wait for the police to tell you?"

"Do you think they'd tell me?" Edda snapped.

"You'll be pleased to know no one was seriously hurt this morning," Delia interrupted.

"And you couldn't take it as a sign to stop interfering?"

"I thought you were trying to protect me."

"Not if you're throwing your life away like this!" David tossed his napkin on the table. "Edda! When will you understand that this is police business, not yours!"

"David, please! Don't do this to me!"

"To you? What about me? I've been in jail, Edda, and it's not something I want to repeat. Hell, I never expected that it would ever happen!"

"They're not pressing charges, so stop worrying."

"Stop worrying? Are you listening to yourself?"

"David, please. I need you. Just as I need Delia. I'm in a community that I barely know. I need your friendship to stop myself from going crazy."

"Edda, you're putting me in a dilemma here. I know I said I wanted to protect you, but I was talking about you being a lesbian. This has nothing to do with that. You've been to the hospital twice already and it's only been a few weeks. Drop it before it kills you."

"But, David—"

"No buts, Edda. When will you realize that it won't bring June back?"

"This has nothing to do with June."

"Doesn't it?" David stared at her.

"Something is going on. We need to know what it is."

"Well I, for one, don't. The police are now involved and that's all I need to know. Call me when you're ready to drop this nonsense." David stood and turned to Delia. "Good night, Delia."

"Good night." Delia said quietly as David walked to the front door.

"David!" Edda called as the front door slammed shut.

"That went well," Delia murmured. "Why couldn't you just keep the information to yourself?"

"I didn't want any lies between us."

"And look where that got you." Delia pushed back from the table and stood.

"Please, don't go. I won't mention it again," Edda pleaded. Delia trudged into the kitchen. "Where are you going?"

"I'm making coffee."

Edda breathed a sigh of relief. At least Delia was still there. It seemed David had drawn the line in the sand and, unless she was prepared to not cross it, she was on her own.

A couple of minutes later Delia returned with two mugs. She passed one to Edda and sat down with hers.

"So what now?"

Delia had a point. "What now? I have absolutely no idea."

"Maybe you should do what David suggested. Drop it."

"It's not about June," Edda said with conviction.

"Isn't it? You said you saw lights but no one else has reported it. Couldn't you have been imagining it? Maybe you thought it was June contacting you."

It was something Edda had thought about. Had she subconsciously not let go of the idea? "I admit the thought had crossed my mind, but what about the other evidence?"

"What other evidence?"

"A grave had been dug up recently and there was wax on one of the headstones."

"Kids. This area is notorious for kids' pranks. Heck, the cemetery is a known make-out spot."

"Kids digging up a grave? That seems a bit over the top, even for delinquents."

"It was probably a dare. Teenage boys are all pricks, you know that."

Edda chuckled. "You're probably right." But Edda doubted she would end her investigation any time soon. There was still the problem of the second body in the coffin. The image of the decomposing body came to mind and she felt her stomach turn.

"Are you all right. You look a little pale."

"Probably something disagreed with me."

"Maybe I should go…" Delia stood and grabbed the two mugs.

"Do you have to?" Edda wasn't quite ready to be alone.

"It's getting late."

It was a weak excuse and they both knew it. The clock on the wall said ten before nine.

"Do you have to work tomorrow?"

"No, but I have chores at home."

"How about we go somewhere for lunch? My treat."

"I don't think it's a good idea."

"Why not? What's wrong with friends having lunch together?" Edda's brow wrinkled.

"Because people will talk." Delia disappeared into the kitchen and returned for the remaining dishes.

"Talk about what?"

When Delia returned for a second time she answered, "You can be an idiot sometimes. What do you think I'm talking about?"

"We're just a couple of girlfriends… oh." Edda glanced at Delia who bit her lip. "Is it going to be uncomfortable?"

"Look, it doesn't worry me because we're just friends, but you're grieving and probably don't need the aggravation. After all, you made that point perfectly clear to me."

"I get your point, Delia, but I'd really like the company. It gets so lonely here and I've run out of conversation with the cat."

"Speaking of which, where is he?" Delia looked around. "He's probably hiding because of me."

"Sorry about that. I don't know what's wrong with him. He's normally very friendly."

"He was June's cat, wasn't he?"

"Yes. How did you know?"

"Just a guess."

"If you don't want to do lunch, how about going with me on my morning walk?"

"It seems a pretty dangerous pastime to me."

"It was an accident."

"That's not what you said before."

Edda gave up trying to talk Delia into coming over. "Thanks for coming by tonight."

Delia looked at her. She tried not to wriggle under Edda's steady gaze. "Fine. What time is your walk?"

"How about eight? Then it won't take up too much of your day."

Delia put her coat on. She grabbed her bag and rummaged around inside for her car keys. "Eight."

Edda didn't want to see her go but she couldn't stop her from leaving, short of fainting on the spot. That thought momentarily crossed her mind and she was so tempted to pull the stunt so Delia would stay a little longer. "Hang on." Edda walked into the kitchen and found her wallet. She pulled out a couple of twenties. "Here." She handed the money to Delia.

"What's that for?"

"Dinner. It was my invitation, remember?"

"Don't be silly."

"Delia, I'm sure you need it more than I do. Errr…I didn't mean…jus…just take it, okay?" Edda shoved the bills into Delia's open bag and tucked her free hand in her jeans pocket. "I wasn't trying to make any social or personal comment, all right? Oh Jesus, why don't I just shut up?"

Delia smiled and air blew out her nose in a sort of snicker. "I'll take it in your normal fumbling way. Only you, my dear Edda, can make an offer sound like a declaration of war."

Edda watched Delia leave and she slowly closed the door as her car disappeared down the street. Whether it was the drugs wearing off or Delia's departure, Edda suddenly felt the full force of being alone. She was sore, she was tired, and had no one to commiserate with.

"Jasper?" The cat had been conspicuously absent during Delia's visit and couldn't be found. She found her bag and dug around inside for the packet of pills the hospital gave her. They had warned that the drugs would knock her out, and she was tempted to do just that, but she was also edgy. Maybe she could make use of the time. Her work was at the point that she needed both hands to continue, so she settled for using the Internet. Maybe it was time to start answering all those emails she had put off.

Chapter Fourteen

The next morning, Edda woke to the sound of the front doorbell. She looked at the time. "Oh, shit!" It was eight o'clock and her mind was still foggy with drugs. "Just a minute!" she hollered.

The doorbell rang twice more before she staggered down the stairs and opened the door.

Delia looked at her with amusement. "Wake you?"

"Sorry. Come in." She stepped aside and let her in. "Give me a moment to finish dressing."

"Those pain medications can knock you around," Delia said knowingly.

"So I'm finding out." Edda hesitated on the bottom step. "Please make yourself at home. You know where the coffeemaker is."

"Is that a hint you want a coffee?" Delia grinned cheekily, exposing her dimples.

"Only if you want a cup of tea."

"I can live without it. Can you?"

Edda gave her a wry smile before she continued up the stairs. She dressed quickly and put aside her normal morning ritual. There was no point in tempting Delia to back out of the exercise. She slipped on her sneakers and clumsily tied up the laces. For better or worse, she was ready.

Edda descended the stairs to the smell of brewing coffee. She followed the scent to its source and found Delia preparing her tea. "Ahh, just what the doctor ordered."

"I'm sure he didn't," Delia responded.

"But that makes it all the more enjoyable."

"Going against doctor's orders?" Delia stirred the tea with her spoon.

"Sinful, isn't it?" Edda poured herself a cup and hummed seductively at the aroma. The tinkling sound Delia's spoon made against her cup stopped and Edda looked up. "What?"

Delia had a strange look on her face. She snapped out of it and answered, "Nothing." She started stirring again and focused her attention on the cup.

"Well, hurry up and drink your tea. We've got a few blocks to cover."

"How many is few?"

"Just thinking of that now?" Edda laughed. "Don't worry. I won't kill you on your first outing."

"First?" Delia looked at her doubtfully. "Only."

Edda kept her mouth shut and drank her coffee. The matter would rest until their return, then maybe she could entice Delia to take another walk.

After rinsing her cup Edda followed Delia out the front door.

"Which way?"

"Does it matter? The sun is shining and the birds are chirping. It's a beautiful day."

"Are you always this disgustingly cheerful in the morning? I don't think I can take it." Delia endorsed the comment with a grumpy look.

"C'mon slowpoke. To the right." Edda slowed her walk to Delia's meandering. She took the opportunity to show her around the neighborhood, especially where the accident took place.

"The car did that?" Delia's mouth hung open. "You're lucky—"

"—I'm alive. Yes, I know. I ended up nearly under the car. It was close enough I could feel the heat from the radiator on my face." Edda looked at the large hole in the hedge.

"Oh, dear Lord!" Delia stared at the torn foliage. "Maybe you should…"

"Should what?"

"Go home before you get killed."

"And I was just starting to like the place."

Delia stopped. "Is it worth it? Really? I'm being serious here."

"You mean the cemetery?"

"Well, there is that, but no. I'm talking about the reason you left home in the first place and came here. Is it worth the risk for a few weeks of isolation? You could always just not answer the phone."

"I suppose I could, but it's too late now. Lesley is settled in my place and I've told her she can stay."

"Still, get out of Dodge before they gun you down." Delia started walking again.

"Are you trying to get rid of me?"

"I don't like seeing you get hurt, Edda."

"You'll miss me," she answered lightly.

Delia glanced sideways to look at her. "Yes, I will," she whispered.

It was a frank admission, and one Edda felt she shouldn't examine too closely. She wondered if Delia had said more than she intended to so she gave her a chance to ignore what she had said. "Did you say something?"

"No. Must have been the breeze."

Edda let the matter rest and continued on with the walk. She made a point of drawing attention to Tom's house and mentioned his part in the building of the estate. When Delia's gaze drifted away Edda stopped. Delia wasn't interested and maybe she was silently hinting to her that she shouldn't be either.

The walk progressed at a delightfully leisurely pace. Edda kept up the stream of chatter while Delia gasped for air. "I'm…sorry…about this. I'm a…little…out of shape."

How could Edda respond to that without coming across as being critical? "Not out of shape, just a little out of conditioning."

Delia smiled at her. "Trust you to find the most diplomatic answer."

Edda smiled back. She found a bench and stopped, indicating to Delia to sit. When Delia resisted Edda sat herself, patting the space next to her. "Come on. Take a breather."

"What? Not going to crack the whip?"

"It's too nice a day. Maybe tomorrow."

"You wish," Delia muttered as she planted her ass on the seat. Her whispered sigh didn't go unnoticed, but Edda refused to comment. "Wish I'd thought of some water."

"Next time."

"I know how I'm going to feel tomorrow. No next time."

Delia sounded adamant but Edda knew somehow she'd get her friend motivated to go walking with her on a regular basis. Maybe she could try David's sneaky method of convincing her that walking was the lesser of two evils.

"If that's the case, how about I take up the hobby of finding you a date?"

"A…what?" Delia's eyebrows crawled up her forehead. "You can't be serious." Edda felt Delia's shocked stare. "Are you?" She shook her head. "No, no, no, no. I don't want, or need, a date." Delia stood and began to walk away at a rapid pace. "Besides, you don't know anyone here. You can't do that. Please, Edda, don't do that."

Edda rose and caught up with the flustered Delia. "Hey! I was kidding. Don't have a panic attack." Delia's chest heaved and tears filled her eyes. "Don't cry." She steered Delia back to her home by the shortest route. "I think a cup of tea is in order," she proclaimed as her key slid into the front door.

Delia's silence didn't bode well. She had overstepped her boundaries again.

"I need the bathroom."

Edda watched her climb the stairs. "Damn it, Edda…" she muttered, "…you've done it again. Why can't you just keep your big mouth shut?" She walked into the kitchen disgusted with herself. Maybe she should take Delia's advice and just go home.

Five minutes later Delia appeared in the kitchen, her face freshly washed and the evidence of tears gone. "Sorry about that," she murmured.

"My fault. David had tried something similar with me to get me to go walking with him. Obviously that doesn't work with everyone."

"No." Delia accepted the offered mug and took a sip.

Edda sat down opposite her at the kitchen table and waited patiently. Would Delia open up and tell her? *Not easily*, she thought.

Delia glanced up once or twice and saw Edda watching her. "What?"

"Nothing."

"That's not a 'nothing' look. I know what you want."

"What are you expecting to happen by telling me?"

"You'll know."

"And? Is the world going to stop spinning because of that?"

"And I'll be embarrassed."

"I could point out that you know an awful lot about me but I know nothing about you."

"Why is it so important to know? Can't we just leave things as they are?"

"Is that what you want?"

"Yes."

"To leave things as they are." Edda knew it was an ambiguous question, but she left it to Delia to interpret it how she may.

"What are you hoping to achieve?" Delia asked.

"I just want to see my friend happy, that's all."

"It's not that simple."

"Isn't it?"

"I think I've been pretty tolerant of your antics, so cut me some slack."

"Fine, we'll carry on as casual friends."

Edda watched closely as Delia bit her lower lip. It was obviously something that Delia had anguished over for a number of years. Surely, it wasn't something bad like killing her boyfriend. "What happened?" she asked quietly.

Delia put her mug down and ran her hand over her forehead. "It was the nineties. I was still living at home and had a day job. Everything was fine but I knew my mother was hoping I'd move out. She didn't say it, but I knew.

Maybe because if I were in her shoes, that's what I'd be expecting from my child."

"That doesn't sound so bad."

"She was also encouraging me to 'find someone,' as she put it. She wanted me married and out of her hair."

"Maybe she was worried your life was passing you by looking after her," Edda interceded.

"At that time she didn't need looking after. She was perfectly healthy." Delia stared her right in the eye to emphasize the point.

"So, did you find someone?"

"It was disaster after disaster. All the men I dated were assholes and wanted only one thing."

"I hate to tell you, Delia, but all men are like that, even the nice ones. It's in their DNA."

"I know that!" she growled. Delia took another sip of her tea to compose herself. "I do, but some are not so gentle about asking."

"Is that the reason you stopped dating?"

"No. The last one I dated was charming. I should have known then, but I was swept away by his adoration of me. No one had ever been like that."

Edda slid her chair closer and took Delia's hands because she had a feeling that the bad part was about to be revealed.

"We lived together in a small apartment on the other side of town to my mother, which seemed to please us all." Delia looked at their joined hands for a moment before lifting her eyes to Edda. "He was an angry drunk."

Edda had heard enough but it was like watching a train wreck about to happen—she couldn't look away. "And..." she whispered while she squeezed the cold fingers enclosed in hers.

"One night he came back and…oh God! It hurt so much!" Tears rolled down Delia's cheeks and Edda felt an answering wetness down her own.

"He…he…"

"You don't have to tell me."

"He hit me with a belt, with the buckle protruding. I was in the hospital for three weeks, the beating was so bad." Delia unconsciously reached behind to touch her back. "I still have the scars from the buckle."

"Did the police arrest him?"

"He was in prison for five years. But it didn't end there. When he got out he spread the word that he was looking for me. I didn't want to stick around to find out what he wanted so I left my home, my mother, and a job I loved in the middle of the night to find a life elsewhere. He had driven me from my life with words. Even after five years he still controlled my life."

Edda stood and heated up some fresh water. Without asking, she took Delia's cup and went about making another cup of tea. She placed it in front of her friend before taking her seat.

"When did you go home?" She knew Delia had returned to look after her mother.

"Three years after I left I found out he had been killed in a car crash, so I figured it was safe to go home. Mama had become ill and incapacitated, so I took care of her. The rest you know."

Edda sat silently while she digested the story she'd been told. What could she say that wouldn't sound inadequate?

"I'm not going through that again." Delia sat back and drank her tea.

"Understood."

The mood of the morning had been broken and Edda knew trying to continue it would be futile. "Walk with me tomorrow?" she asked hopefully. She knew she'd count herself lucky if Delia talked to her. "I truly am sorry."

"What for? It was his fault, not yours."

"But I went and dragged it all up again."

"Well, now you know."

"Yes, now I know."

Chapter Fifteen

Edda woke up to the loud and intrusive sound of a garbage lid hitting the ground. She lay in bed and listened, waiting to see if it was a random accident by a prowling feline or something she should be worried about. She took the opportunity to go to the bathroom and couldn't stop herself from looking out the window. It was quiet at the cemetery, as it had been for the last few nights.

After the sound of the flushing toilet died down she heard a swish, as if someone had brushed by a bush outside. Coincidence? Edda went back to the bedroom and felt around in the dark for her cell. She gazed at the illuminated bedside clock. Five o'clock. Did she want to call the police and then find out she was a fool if they found nothing? After her previous experience with them she was doubtful they'd believe her. Maybe it was a matter of the girl who cried wolf once too often?

The house was once again silent. Had it been her overactive imagination? Edda sat on the edge of the bed for a few minutes, the cell in her hand. When it appeared her fear was unfounded she clambered back under the covers and put the cell next to the clock. "Stupid." Her final thought as she drifted off to sleep was of Jasper and what she'd do to him if he was responsible for the garbage lid.

However her sleep was short-lived. Someone was at the front door, she was sure of it. She got out of bed and crept along the hallway to the top of the stairs. In the dimness of streetlight-illuminated living room Edda could see the door handle move. Now was the time to make that call.

She found herself back on the edge of her bed, cell in hand, punching in 911. She stopped and hung up. By the time the police arrived the felon would be long gone. Instead she opened the cell phonebook and looked for the one person who could help, if she could convince him to. She wasn't high on his like list, but surely he would help if she was in danger. She dialed the number.

The intruder was now in her house. The door closed and she could hear footsteps.

She listened to the phone ring. "Come on, David," she whispered. A creak from downstairs notched up her apprehension. How long would it take for the intruder to come up the stairs?

She was about to doubt that David would be able to help her when he answered. "Hello?" His sleep-filled voice did little to inspire her.

"David? It's Edda."

"Edda, it's…five a.m."

"I know that, David. I've got an intruder in the house."

"Call the police."

"I need help here." She heard someone coming up the stairs. "He's on the stairs. Please, David."

"Fine. Give me a minute." He didn't sound convinced. Had she been such a nuisance to everyone that no one believed her?

"Hurry." She disconnected the call and placed the cell on the bedside table. Edda hopped into bed and feigned sleep hoping the intruder would take what he wanted then leave.

It didn't take long for him to find her. She could nearly smell his presence in her room so she kept her eyes shut. A far-off rattle of a cupboard door downstairs scared her. Was there a second intruder or was it David? The man in her room didn't seem concerned about the noise and continued to poke around. She had to believe there were two of them. David was now at a serious disadvantage, and she was unable to warn him.

The sound of a key slipping into the front door alerted everyone to David's arrival. The intruder quickly left her room and headed down the hallway. Edda grabbed her cell off the nightstand and called for help.

"911. What is your emergency?"

"Hi, I'm Edda Case and there are two intruders in my house."

"Your address?"

She was about to answer when a voice called from below. "You better get down here, lady, or your friend gets it." It was a crude threat at best, but one she knew she couldn't ignore.

"What's going on there? Where are you located, ma'am?"

She recited the address and hung up. A quick glance around the bedroom revealed nothing useful as a weapon.

"You have five seconds."

She had no choice but to go downstairs weaponless.

"All right. I'm here," she said calmly. She held up her hands as she approached the room with the light on. In the kitchen she found David tied to a chair. A small scrape across his cheekbone seemed to be the only visible wound, so she assumed they hadn't roughed him up too much. She suspected that had been postponed for her to witness.

"Sit." She was grabbed roughly and shoved onto a chair where she was tightly secured with rope.

"What do you want? Just take it and leave."

The older of the two men stood in front of her. "Where is it?"

"Where is what?" Edda glanced at David, who shrugged his shoulders.

"You know. You've taken enough of an interest in it in the past few weeks."

Edda tried to size up her tormentor. He was at least in his forties and had the demeanor of a cruel man. One that was not going to take no for an answer. He sneered at her, grabbed her nightshirt and pulled her closer. "Sooner or later, you *will* tell me."

"I really don't know what you're talking about."

"TELL ME!"

"I...DON'T...KNOW! How many times will I have to tell you? Neither David nor I have any idea what you're talking about."

"Maybe you need some incentive." The man pointed his gun at David and fired. David gave out an agonized cry. "The next one will hit something more vital."

"I've been living here for a couple of months. What am I supposed to know?" She turned her tear-streaked eyes at David. "Are you all right?" She could see he was in pain, and lots of it.

His bottom lip remained tucked under his front teeth. He nodded slowly. The intruder pointed his gun at David and cocked it.

"Stop it!!" she screamed. "We don't know anything!"

"Why don't I believe you?"

"Maybe you should be asking yourself who else knows about this?"

"Don't push me, woman!" He waved his gun around and approached her to shove it at her face. "What do you know?"

"All I know is that I saw a light at the cemetery in the middle of the night and a shovel in the backyard. That's it. You broke in and held us captive."

"You've been snooping around."

"David and I walked to the cemetery and found that the earth had been turned recently. I went to the council to check the plans but they were gone. We both know that this estate sits on the ground of the original cemetery."

"And you know too much," he sneered. "Who else knows?"

"Besides the police…?"

His hand flicked out quickly and caught her across the mouth. "Smack me around all you like. It won't change the fact that they know." For good measure, his hand made a return swipe at her. This blow shoved her cheek onto her tooth and left her with bloodstained lips. Another man entered the back door.

"Did you find anything?"

"There ain't nuthin' there."

Despite the double negative Edda kept her mouth shut. She glanced at David and saw the blood trailing from the bullet wound to his shoulder. Her eyes made contact with his and she smiled grimly. Things were not looking good.

"Looks like someone beat us to it."

The man with the gun turned to face them, his expression tight with anger. "And that's not good for you." He stepped up to Edda and put the muzzle of his gun against her temple. "This is your last chance. Where is it?"

"We don't…" She never got to finish the sentence. He hit her with the butt of the gun and she reeled back from the force.

"Stop it!" David yelled. "We told you before. We don't know anything."

"You knew enough to call in the cops."

"That's because you were intruders in her house, nothing more." The man stepped over to David and pushed his thumb into the wound until he drew an agonized cry.

"How…how old…is…the hole?" Edda slurred. Her head spun and it felt ready to crack open.

"What hole?" the second man asked.

"She means was it dug up recently?" David offered.

"Nope. Grassy and everyfing. Hadn't been touched."

"Make some sense, will ya?"

"I dug where you told me. Ain't nothing there."

"He means—"

"I know what he means. Shut the hell up!"

"Someone…else…" Edda's head throbbed.

The man with the gun stood still for a moment and thought. "Of all the low, scheming…that son of a bitch!"

There was the faint sound of a siren approaching fast.

"Last…chance…" Edda passed out.

✝

She regained consciousness some time later. They had apparently been left alone in the kitchen. Her head throbbed and David's image swam before her eyes.

"Edda? Are you all right?" His voice was strained.

"Where…" Edda's mouth was dry.

He kept his voice low. "They're in a standoff against the police."

Edda blinked once or twice to try and get him in focus. Slowly, her vision obliged her. "How long?" she croaked.

"Don't know. Maybe twenty minutes." He glanced at the door. "Keep your voice down."

"Why?"

"Because they think you're unconscious."

"And?" Edda had no idea what he was talking about.

"And if they don't know that we may have a chance to escape."

Edda tested her bonds. "I don't think so." She looked at the kitchen counter and saw the knife block was empty.

"They took them."

Edda shuffled her chair across the floor.

"What are you doing?"

"Shhhh."

"What are you doing?"

"Do you want us to get caught?" She heard a scuff of boots and dropped her head.

"What are you up to?" The second man asked.

He prodded Edda and David spoke. "She's still unconscious."

"Don't do nufin' stupid." Content that his words would have the desired effect, he left them alone again.

"As if..." Edda muttered. She continued her slow journey across the floor to a drawer. The chair rotated slowly as she lined up her hands with the handle. After a number of attempts, she managed to pry open the drawer. Inside were her work implements and, more importantly, her leather knife. The wickedly curved knife was dangerously sharp and she handled it with the respect she knew it had earned. It was hard work and the sweat on her brow slid down into her eyes.

She shook her head and instantly regretted it. The room swayed and rolled as she desperately held on to her conscious state. The knife became slippery in her sweaty hands and it nicked her skin. The warm fluid painted her fingers red and made the job even harder.

Edda took a deep breath and focused on the rope binding her wrists. She guided the knife by touch and slowly drew it across her bonds. When there was no immediate pain she brought it back and pushed it forward again, this time with more force. It took a minute to saw through its width and every muscle in her body ached when the restriction was removed.

"Jimmy!"

It sounded like the standoff had escalated and Edda had to move fast. Despite her head wound she stood and moved to David, wielding the knife competently to cut the rope quickly. "Let's get out of here."

The young accomplice had been alerted to their escape. "Hey!"

"Out! Now!" Edda was already on her way to the back door when the second man entered the kitchen. David threw himself at him. They rolled around on the floor, the man's gun skittering across the kitchen and out of reach.

"David!" she whispered harshly.

His fist shot out and caught the man on the chin. David took the opportunity to run.

Both made it out the back door as the leader entered the kitchen. He fired his gun and a chip flew out of the doorframe. Neither of them stopped, running to the side fence. David locked his fingers together and gave Edda a foothold. She had barely gotten on when he shoved her over the fence.

"Help!" Edda yelled as loud as she could.

"Get back here!" The man stood with his gun trained on David's back.

"Drop your weapon!"

Two policemen appeared in David's backyard, their guns drawn. They climbed up to where they could get a good view of Edda's backyard. She looked over the fence and found the two gunmen surrounded by half a dozen police, each one yelling "drop it!" or "no sudden moves!" or "put your hands up!"

By the look on the second gunman's face, he was trying to decide which order to obey first. The leader, however, seemed more experienced in such matters and did as they all asked.

"Are you okay?" Edda asked.

An exhausted David smiled. "I was about to ask you the same thing."

"I'm fi—" She then passed out for the second time in an hour.

Chapter Sixteen

"God! Are you all right?"

Edda's head throbbed heavily. She opened her eyes slowly to see Delia hovering over her. "Where…" Her voice cracked and her throat stung.

"You're safe in the hospital. You really do need a nanny." Edda eyeballed Delia grumpily. "Well, you do. You can't seem to keep yourself out of trouble."

Edda felt Delia's cool fingertips at her wrist. Content with her comforting presence, Edda closed her eyes and allowed Delia to do her observations.

"Da-vid." The two syllables slipped clumsily from her lips.

"He's fine. After the doctor has seen you I'll get him for you."

"Thanks."

Delia let go of her wrist and Edda missed the contact. She forced her eyes open and tried to focus on her at the end of her bed. "When?"

"You've been out for three days."

"Threeeee," Edda slurred.

"The doctor kept you sedated to allow your brain to recover. This is your second knock to the head in a month, Edda. I might have to buy you a helmet or something."

As it was, her head felt like a large kettle drum, so she couldn't begin to imagine how it would have felt three days ago.

"How's the head?" The owner of the new voice appeared in the doorway.

"She's just awakened, Doctor."

He walked over to Delia, took the chart out of her hands and scanned the results. He moved to Edda's bed and took out a penlight. He shone it into her eyes. "Headache?"

"God, yes." Edda resisted the urge to grab her head.

He wrote on her chart. "She can have two painkillers now. No more than four times daily. No food until tomorrow."

"Yes, Doctor."

Edda suddenly realized that she had an IV in her arm. In a way she was glad she didn't have to eat because she thought she would throw it all back up.

"That's quite a bruise you've got." He prodded the bruise in question until Edda was ready to slap him if he didn't stop. When she glared at him he grinned at her and removed his hand. "Get some rest."

Edda mentally rolled her eyes. The man was the master of understatement. She closed her eyes and hoped he would go away. She counted to ten and reopened her eyes, glad to see that the room was empty. A few seconds later Delia appeared with a small cup and a glass of water.

"Can you sit up?" Delia put down the medication and helped Edda to sit.

"I don't feel so good." Edda lay still and waited for the nausea to subside.

Delia stood there and watched her closely. "You okay?"

Edda couldn't answer. Her stomach hurt, her mouth had a nasty aftertaste and her head pounded. "Kill me now." When the pounding subsided to a dull ache she asked, "Why are you here?"

"I have to make sure you don't do something silly."

"Uh-huh." It was all too much. Edda closed her eyes and tried to relax.

Edda allowed Delia to fuss around her. She wasn't aware of nodding off, but the last thing she remembered was the scent of Delia's freshly scrubbed body drifting around her and the faint aroma of antiseptic cleaner.

†

When Edda woke the same smell hung around her. "Delia?" Edda heard the scrape of a chair on the floor.

"How are you feeling?" Delia's low voice was soothing.

"Like shit."

Delia chuckled. "Why am I not surprised?"

"Wha...happ...?" Edda's brain felt like mush.

"The doctor gave you a little something to help you sleep."

"How long?"

"A couple of days."

Edda opened her eyes slowly. It was way too bright and she closed them again.

"Sorry. Not a lot I can do about the light."

"S'kay." She felt her hand lifted and placed, she assumed, in Delia's hand.

"How's the head?"

She stuck out her tongue and heard another snicker.

She opened her eyes a bit and saw Delia standing next to her. "How long have you been here?" she whispered.

179

Delia's gaze wandered. "A little while."

But Edda suspected she wasn't telling the complete truth. Delia's clothes looked rumpled. "Why didn't you go home?"

"I went home." Edda remained silent. "Well, someone had to keep an eye on you in case you had an accident again."

Edda heard Delia's defensiveness in her voice and she suspected that Delia would deny anything more.

"You've been a good friend." Her head began to pulse angrily with pain. "Can I have something for a headache?"

"Sure."

A moment later she heard the sound of footsteps.

"Yes, ma'am?"

"The patient has woken up. She's asked for pain medication."

"Right away." The footsteps receded.

"Ma'am?" Edda croaked. "Hah!" She coughed.

"I outrank her."

"They'll talk."

"Let 'em. I don't care."

"Delia…"

"Now is not the time. You're ill and I'm doing my job." Delia fussed over the pillows. "You'll have to sit up for the pills." Edda felt half the bed rise to move her to a semi-seated position. Without asking, Delia slipped her arm under Edda's body and gently pulled her up in the bed. Edda's hands went out to support herself on the mattress and she pushed as hard as her headache would allow. A dart of pain shot through her injured wrist but she pushed it to the back of her mind. Her throbbing head far outranked a fading wrist sprain.

The nurse returned with the small container and Delia poured a glass of water from the water jug beside the bed.

"There you go." She handed over the pills and steadied the glass for Edda to drink.

Edda felt her stomach churning but she wasn't sure whether it was hunger or nausea.

"There's someone here who would like to see you before he's discharged."

"David?"

"Not unless you have a second neighbor named David tucked away somewhere."

Edda looked up at her. "Thanks."

"He's still waiting for the doctor to give him the all clear, then there's paperwork and medication. I'll send him in when that's done and by then your pain pills will have had time to work."

"Thanks." Edda squeezed Delia's hand and observed her response. "And you should go home and get some rest." She could see the hesitation in Delia's demeanor. "I think I'll survive now."

"Are you sure?" But Delia didn't make any immediate move to leave.

Edda could see that she was beyond tired and suspected that Delia had been doing triple duty to keep an eye on her. "I'll probably sleep." Delia's small frown didn't go unnoticed. "Unless, of course, you want to stay," Edda added.

"Do you want me to stay?" she asked hopefully.

Edda was caught in a dilemma. Obviously Delia needed some rest but something told her their relationship was slowly sliding away from friendship toward something she was pretty sure she wasn't ready for. She looked into those pretty, pretty eyes and felt herself giving an answer from her heart. "Sure, but you need a bed, a shower, and some food, not necessarily in that order." Delia seemed conflicted. "Go on. I'll still be here when you get back."

"Promise?"

"I promise, unless the doctor kicks me out, and that's unlikely to happen any time soon. When are you next back on duty?"

"Tomorrow."

"Well then—"

"I know. I know. Go home."

Edda watched her leave then settled back on her pillow. The pain medication slowly put her into a state of dull agony. What only seemed a few moments but had to be, in fact, an hour later, she awoke to the sound of knocking on the door.

"Hey, stranger." Despite his injury David seemed in good spirits.

Edda tried to focus on him but his image was blurred. "Hey," she said groggily.

"How's the head?" He sat down in the visitor's chair, nudging the sling on his arm into a more comfortable position.

"How's...the shoulder?" Edda tried to shift further up the pillow.

"I asked first."

Edda poked out her tongue and David laughed, which made her even more pissed off. "You've been shot so stop being so cheerful!"

"The stuff they gave me is great! I don't feel a thing."

"I hope you're not driving."

"My car is back at the house, remember? Nope, a taxi for me." He grabbed the glass on the bedside table and offered it to Edda. "When are they letting you out?"

"Probably never. The conversation hasn't even gotten around to that subject yet."

"Yikes. I better feed that mangy old cat of yours."

"Thanks." She looked at David seriously. "Thanks for coming to my rescue."

"Sorry I wasn't much help." He sounded disappointed.

"Don't think you didn't do anything." Edda suddenly felt guilty for all those times she wished David had been somewhere else than in her life. "You risked your life to save mine."

A small smile touched his lips. "Yeah?" he said almost shyly.

"Your brother would be proud of you."

His head dropped and he nodded solemnly. Edda reached out with difficulty, but she persisted until she had a firm grip of his arm. She tugged until he relented and moved his hand over to hers. "Thank you." She had never said those two words and meant it as sincerely as she did then.

"Speaking of police, they came and saw me a couple of days ago for a statement."

"Did they tell you anything?"

"Detective Wilson…Watson…"

"Webber," Edda corrected.

"Yeah, Webber. He said those guys had just been let out of jail after twelve years for armed robbery. It seems the getaway driver had been let out ten years ago and came looking for the cash. They'd stashed it in one of the coffins for safe keeping."

"Ahhh." Edda's interest was piqued. "So the driver signed on to the construction crew and raided the coffin in the move to the field. Makes sense. That would explain the lights I've been seeing. Those guys were trying to find the cash."

"That's the funny thing. These guys had only been released a few days ago."

"A few days? Then that means…"

"…it wasn't them."

"So, does that mean I'm still crazy?"

"They were able to identify the remains in the coffin. It was the driver."

"But somebody had to bury him. Right?"

David remained silent.

"Right?"

"Yeah." He sighed deeply and Edda knew what it meant. His disapproval.

"Look. I'm sure the cops realize there is someone out there who is guilty of murder and they'll do their best to solve it."

David stared at her like she had two heads.

"Don't look at me like that. I feel like shit so I'm not up to any sleuthing in the near future. By then, they should have their man, woman, or child."

He shook his head. "I never thought I'd hear you say that."

"Me either, but my head hurts and my stomach feels like I'm going to puke. At present I couldn't care less about a murder. However, I may change my mind in a couple of days so take notice now. You may not hear it again."

"Now *that* I believe."

Chapter Seventeen

Despite her belief that she would be stuck in a hospital bed forever, Edda was released three days later. Scans had been normal and besides a residual queasiness her recovery had progressed well. It was only Delia's assurance that she would call in each day to check up on her that convinced the doctor to let her leave.

Now home, Edda was able to relax. Hospitals reminded her too much of June. Too many hospitals. Too many doctors. Too many treatments. Too many memories. Delia fussed around her and made her comfortable on the sofa. When she was satisfied she disappeared into the kitchen and made coffee.

Edda lay quietly with her eyes closed, drifting toward sleep. She jumped when a furry body landed on her. "Geezus!" she croaked. Jasper looked directly down at her face, his body firmly seated on her chest.

"Meow."

"You say that now…" Edda couldn't decide whether to shove him off or leave him be. Jasper made the decision for her and curled up on her chest, his head dropping to his paws. He purred loudly and she smiled. "Good to see you too. Sorry I haven't been home much lately."

"What is that cat doing here?" Delia's voice caught her off guard and she jumped. Jasper extended his claws to keep from falling off his human pillow. Edda winced as the claws found purchase through her clothes. Delia waved her hand at him. "Get off!"

"It's okay. Let him be."

"Fine. Then you can drink your coffee through a straw."

"Coffee?" She inhaled and smelled the familiar aroma. "Sorry, Jasper." No cat was going to stand between her and the mug. She lifted him off her chest and deposited him on the floor. Before she could make an effort to move a firm hand grabbed her arm and helped her to sit upright. Edda looked up into Delia's eyes. "Thanks."

Delia answered her with a nod. While Edda drank her coffee she could see something was bothering her friend. "What's wrong?"

"Nothing. Why?" Delia busied herself with her tea, constantly sipping the liquid. It was a delaying tactic and they both knew it.

"Because you're as nervous as a teenager in a room full of crying babies." She watched Delia play with her mug. "Let me help you."

Delia's eyes slowly rose and met hers. "Even if it is about you?"

"Oh. Well, then I'm an authority on the subject."

"You may not want to know."

"That you're interested in me?" Edda waited for Delia's response. She already knew the answer to that.

"I…errr…how did you know?" Delia's face turned the shade of a sun-kissed apple.

"Come on. You were with me nonstop at the hospital and now you're nursing me at home?"

"I'm just conscientious."

"Yes you are, but you've also got a vested interest in me."

"You're very calm about this."

"Delia...sweet Delia. I'm sick not blind."

"So?" she asked hopefully.

Edda looked down into the depths of her mug. I..." How could she put into words what she didn't understand herself? "Look"

"That's okay. I suspected as much."

The crestfallen look was almost Edda's undoing.

"No one ever wants me."

Edda grabbed Delia's arm before she made a run for it. "Whoa there, young lady!"

"I'm not young."

"To me, you are." Edda yanked on her arm when Delia tried to stand. "Sit down. I'll try to explain."

"No need to explain. I don't want to hear why not." Delia struggled against Edda's firm grip.

"Look. I like you, Delia. I like you a lot. But inside here..." she tapped her chest, "... are a whole lot of memories and guilt that I'm not ready to come to terms with yet."

Delia stopped resisting.

"I know it's not fair to you, but it's the only answer I have for now."

"Are you sticking around?"

"I can't say that I've given it much thought lately." Edda watched Delia's face and saw the emotional shutters drop. "But, I've been rather busy in that time." Edda's gaze scanned the room. "It has been nice here, though. I think I could get used to it." There was a glimmer of hope in Delia's eyes. "It may not be up to me. If Lesley wants more time I'd say I'll be here a while longer."

"When will you know that?"

"When I call her, I suppose." Delia's eyes roamed the room and Edda knew exactly what she was looking for. "She's still at work."

"Huh?" Another blush rose up Delia's face.

"I know you want me to put you out of your misery, but Lesley is still at work. I'll talk to her. I promise." Edda finished her coffee and put the mug on the small side table next to the sofa. "Now, if you'll excuse me, I have a few things—"

"Oh, no. You stay put. Doctor's orders."

"But—"

"No buts either. What do you need to do?" Delia had already stood and removed Edda's mug.

"Just some housework."

"There's blood on this floor," Delia called from the kitchen.

"Probably mine."

"We can't have that. Where's the mop?"

"Errr…can't remember." She felt it was better than saying I have no clue.

Delia emerged from the kitchen. "You have no idea, do you?"

Edda looked at her sheepishly. "Errr…"

"Enough said." Edda could just hear the muffled comments from her visitor as she left. She picked up *a breeding ground for germs* and *wasn't born with the brains God gave her*, muttered in disgust. She suppressed a smile and lay her head back against the sofa. Was this going to be the story of her life for the next few days, or even weeks? Was she prepared to share her personal space with someone she'd only met a few weeks ago?

For now, according to the doctor, she had no option but to accept the help graciously.

†

The next week and a half had been spent practically immobile. Edda hadn't realized how ingrained her walking regime had become in her life until she couldn't do it, and it was making her cranky.

Delia dutifully came every day to check up on her, sometimes for a couple of hours sometimes only minutes, depending on her work schedule. Edda found herself waiting in anticipation of Delia's next visit.

Edda took the opportunity the downtime provided to finish her commission, and she was well-pleased with the outcome. Now that it was done it was up to Barbara. While Karen was her assistant, Barbara was the goddess who transformed her ideas into reality. Barbara was the one who could approve or reject Edda's designs, if what she wanted was physically impossible to do. The only sticking point she could see was the leather weave, but Barbara was resourceful and she rarely said no and Edda was under no illusion that Barbara sometimes sent out work she was incapable of doing herself. So far her confidentiality had been impeccable so she had no qualms about using Barbara's services.

She packed up Daniel's portfolio and her own contributions to the project into a box and sealed it. The work was now in Barbara's, and Karen's, hands.

†

After ten days of being housebound Edda could finally go outside and, more importantly, she could once again take her daily stroll around the estate. With Delia beside her, she

189

ventured out for a short walk. At Delia's insistence Edda took it slow, starting out by walking to the end of the block then returning home. It wasn't until later that first day on her own that she understood the wisdom of Delia's advice. Edda was ready for bed after having something simple for dinner.

Edda checked her watch before she reached for her cell and punched in a familiar number. "Tamara?"

"Edda, love. Good to hear your voice. How are you?"

"Fine." She wasn't going to bring up the run of bad luck she'd had recently. While Tamara was her agent, and a good friend, word would soon get around and by the time the news got back to her it would inevitably have evolved into something more, like she was dead or dismembered. She never underestimated the power of gossip. "I'm calling to let you know you can send Karen."

"Are you finished already? Wow!" Tamara sounded impressed.

"A few days ago, but it's only the first stage, my dear. I want the package to go to Barbara."

"Barbara? Do you think that's wise?"

"Barbara has worked for me for over ten years, you know that. I trust her."

"Well, if you say so."

"I *do* say so. She's a very talented woman and she's used to my scribble. I need her to check that what I've designed will work. I don't want the finished product to fail at Daniel's moment of triumph."

"It won't do that."

"It shouldn't but I don't want to take any chances. Not now. Besides, we have a little time to spare."

"All right, if that's what you want."

"I want. Can you call Barbara for me and tell her it's on its way? And give her a deadline date." Edda knew very well she should have made the call herself, but she wasn't ready to face the people in her old life just yet. Reluctantly she added, "Tell her I'll call in the next few days."

"Does this mean you're open for business?"

Edda could hear the hope in Tamara's voice. "Not yet. I'll let you know when I'm ready."

"But—"

"Daniel is special, Tam. I did it as a favor."

"But you still get paid. Right?"

Edda bit her tongue. She wanted to say mind your own business but it *was* her business. "Yes, Daniel is very generous." Edda usually handled Daniel herself and didn't involve Tamara in the details of the project. Tam begrudgingly understood that but this time she was involved and Edda had to go over the arrangements she had with her oldest customer. "Now, stop worrying."

"All right, it's your dime."

"When can I expect Karen?" Edda had already assumed her assistant would be the courier.

"I'll check with her and get back to you."

She knew Karen was angling for a couple of days off so Edda kept her mouth shut. She was doing her a favor by driving out to pick up the work and Edda felt that Karen deserved the break. "Fine."

"Anything else?"

"Nope. That's it. It felt strange doing this without…J-June leaning over my shoulder." She stumbled over her lover's name.

"Things will get better in time."

"I know." She didn't really want to discuss it. "Call me when you're ready."

"Sure thing. Are you sure…?"

"I'm fine, Tam. Goodbye." Edda hung up before Tam pushed and prodded her into having a heart-to-heart. Funny, she'd been able to talk to David and Delia about it, but talking about it to anyone from her previous life had been off limits. Was it the fact that neither of them had a vested interest in her past, and so could approach June's passing with some level of objectivity, or were her two new friends the bridge between her old and new life? Either way, Edda felt a level of relaxation with them she couldn't feel around her old friends just yet.

After she completed the call Edda looked at her watch and sighed. It had been a long day and she was ready for bed. Maybe tomorrow wouldn't turn out to be so exhausting.

†

Day by day Edda's stamina increased, and each day her walk took her a little further toward her goal of returning to full fitness. Delia tagged along and was delighted by the shorter outings, so Edda accepted that, for now, she was restricted to short walks around the block with her friend. If that's what it took to settle into a comfortable arrangement, then so be it.

Inevitably, the day came that Delia's shift work clashed with their walk and Edda was left to walk alone. The neighborhood was the same and the weather was favorable, but somehow the walk wasn't the same. She had come to rely on Delia's presence more than she realized and all she could think was that it was too soon.

"Too soon for what?" she muttered to herself. But she didn't answer. It wasn't an answer she wanted to give.

Edda's week dragged by as her life returned to the humdrum of sitting around reading books. Her work was done and with Karen's arrival on Friday it would be out of her hands, and with the crime already solved she had nothing else to pique her interest. Maybe another hobby was needed.

†

Karen's car roared into the driveway with its usual noisiness. Edda stepped out onto the stoop to meet her.

"You know, you'd save gas if you didn't keep revving it," she yelled over the racing engine.

The engine stopped and the ensuing silence was deafening. Karen got out of her car and went to the trunk to gather her bag. "If I don't, it stalls."

Edda was pleased to see that Karen was a bit more relaxed this time and didn't leave her bag in the car for a quick escape. She stepped aside to let her visitor enter before her. "How's things back home?" Home? Was that true anymore?

"Hectic as ever. I had a couple of old customers asking after you, wondering what you were up to and, more to the point, if you were still in business." Karen dropped her bag at the bottom of the stairs before moving through the living room into the kitchen. When Edda didn't answer immediately, Karen continued, "Are you?"

Edda opened a cupboard and took out two mugs. She thought seriously about the question and about the last few days of inactivity. It was doubtful she could stand day after day of doing very little. Whether she liked it or not she needed to work, even though money wasn't the issue. It was more her state of mind. "I suppose I am, but I don't want to jump back into the workload I had before…June's death. I'll have to rely on Tamara's judgment to choose which assignments are important." Karen gave her a wry look as an opinion of Tamara's decision-making.

"Come on. You know she's very good at what she does. Be nice," Edda said as she pottered around the kitchen, gathering a jar of cookies. She took a seat across the table from her assistant and pushed one mug over. "So…what's new?"

"Much the same. Petro has put out a new line."

"He's pushing to get his name out there," Edda conceded.

"He's trying to take your market share," Karen replied.

"Is he succeeding?" Edda tried to sound unconcerned about the state of the market, but she had spent too many years in the industry worrying about it not to.

Karen waggled her hand. "Hard to tell. You're going to need something spectacular to get back on top."

Did she want to, as Karen put it, get back on top? "I'd be happy for steady employment."

"You know there's always that offer from Sienna."

Months ago Edda had been approached by a large retail chain to design exclusive bag wear for them. At the time she had been too wrapped up in June's illness to care and had declined. Did she really want her work to be vetoed by an administrator? Her artistic freedom had always been something she cherished. Did she still think that? The thought of her designs being mass produced and sold at a discounted price she felt cheapened her reputation.

"I don't think I want to go there. Always be on a timetable. How can you create to a deadline?"

Karen regarded her. "Do I point out that this current project is to a deadline? However, it seems you've made you mind up."

"Yes, it does."

"When are you coming home?"

That was a harder question to answer. "I don't know. I'm not even sure I want to go home." Edda's gaze casually shifted around the kitchen as she answered.

"I hope you're not expecting me to come out here every week."

"If I decide to stay, we'll make some sort of arrangement with a courier that won't get Tamara's thong in a knot."

Karen chuckled. "Now that's an image." Karen sipped her coffee and reached for a cookie. "Why do you want to stay? I thought this was temporary."

"I don't know. It's just...a slower pace than the apartment. More relaxed. More real."

"Real?" Karen took a bite of the cookie.

"It's so different from my old life, Karen, and I think it's something that I need right now."

"It's because of June," Karen commented bluntly before she realized what she had said. "Sorry."

"Don't be sorry. I think you're right. I don't need the added stress right now, at least not until my head is in the right place."

"So it looks like you're staying. Do you want me to tell Tamara?"

"No, leave that to me. She's not going to like it." Edda saw that Karen had finished her coffee and was content to just hold the empty mug in her hands. "Would you like to freshen up?"

"I could use some downtime." Karen stood and took the mug to the sink. "Same room?"

"Yup. Dinner will be about six, if that's okay."

"Sure."

Karen walked away and left Edda alone in the kitchen. She sat there for a moment longer and considered the conversation. It seemed she had made her decisions for her life in Lesley's home without too much thought, but did she mean it?

Chapter Eighteen

The meal went as planned. That was until the front doorbell rang. Edda hadn't been expecting Delia, but she was sure she could offer her something in the way of dinner if need be. However, the person at the door was someone who had been absent in her life of late.

"David! What are you doing here?"

He stood there with a bouquet of roses in his hand. "Can I come in?"

"Sure." Edda stepped aside and let David in. She was about to say he shouldn't have bought the flowers, but luckily her hesitation saved her from embarrassment.

"Hi, Karen. These are for you." Karen dropped her cutlery when David handed over the flowers. "I saw your car in the driveway."

That, at least, answered the question for Edda. "We were just having dinner. Do you want to join us?" She knew the answer even before she asked it.

"Why sure. I'd love to." David's gaze never left Karen's face. He sat down in the vacant seat next to her and continued the conversation. "You didn't call. Did you get my messages?"

"Sorry, David, I've been busy. You know how it is." Karen stuck the flowers under her nose and breathed in deeply. "But thanks for the roses."

Yeah, I know how it is, Edda thought. Poor David had been shot down before he even had a chance to take off.

"Let me take those," Edda offered and headed to the kitchen to put the flowers in water. "Damn it," she muttered. This was one time she wished she didn't know Karen as well as she did. Grabbing the bottle of wine and a glass, Edda returned to the dining room and poured a glass for David. "Here you go. I'll just rustle up some dinner for you."

David didn't hear her because his whole attention was on Karen. Edda shook her head and put what remained of the dinner preparations onto a plate and microwaved it. Should she warn David or let things play themselves out? No, he wouldn't appreciate her interfering but, on the other hand, she couldn't just stand by and let this train wreck happen either. She took out the hot plate and utensils and placed them in front of her love-struck friend.

"Eat up before it gets cold."

David gave her a warm smile. "Thanks. So what have you two been up to?"

"Catching up on work news. You know, that sort of thing," Edda said, but she felt she was talking to herself. "Don't mind me."

"What about you, Karen?" David cut his meat and placed a forkful into his mouth.

Edda braced herself for Karen's reply.

"Edda keeps me pretty busy." Karen looked at Edda and dared her to say otherwise.

"Seven days a week? Edda, how could you."

"I…I…"

"She's catching up on the backlog of work. Isn't that right?"

"May I talk to you in the kitchen please?" Edda stood and waited for Karen to do the same. She grabbed her elbow and pushed her through the doorway. When she felt she was far enough away from David for him not to hear she hissed, "What do you think you're doing?"

"Nothing."

"You and I both know that's a lie. Why don't you just tell him the truth?"

"What truth?"

Edda felt her anger rise. "Stop this. If you don't want to go out with him just tell him. Stop playing games."

"But Edda, he looks at me with those puppy eyes! How can I resist that?"

David's voice called out from the dining room. "Is everything all right?"

Edda and Karen called out in unison "Yes!"

"If he asks you to go out with him tomorrow you'll accept."

"But—"

"If you still feel the same way tomorrow tell him then. He is a sweet man and doesn't deserve you stringing him along. Now, get back in there and make conversation with him. Do you understand me?"

Karen stared at her and Edda half expected her to rebel. She opened her mouth then closed it again. "Okay," she said meekly.

David looked up from his meal as they entered the dining room. "Okay?"

"Everything's fine, isn't it Karen?" Edda glared at her across the table.

"Yeah. Sure. Fine." Karen dug into her food with gusto.

"So, David," Edda prompted, "what are you doing tomorrow?"

"Nothing. Why?"

Karen shook her head vigorously while David's attention was on Edda, but it abruptly stopped when he turned his head.

"It's supposed to be a beautiful day. Why don't you two lovebirds go on a picnic?"

Karen's lips thinned, letting Edda know what she thought of that idea and, Edda knew, especially the reference to lovebirds.

"Hey! That's not a bad idea. How about I pick you up around eleven?"

Edda observed the interaction between them and knew she was butting in, just as she promised herself she wouldn't, but she had to force Karen's hand to make the girl come clean.

"Yeah, that'll be great," Karen said in a monotone.

Edda smiled inwardly. Karen was not happy, and she knew she'd hear about it once David had left. But she wasn't sorry she did it. Someone had to see the whole picture and she was it.

†

David finally left after some not-so-subtle prodding from Edda. He was determined to squeeze out as much face-to-face time as he could get with Karen, and it wasn't until she pointed out he still had tomorrow with her that he finally caved in and left.

Seconds after the door closed Karen growled at her, "What did you do that for?"

"Don't you want to go out with him?" Edda said sweetly, knowing that Karen was shooting daggers at her.

"No! Yes! I don't know!" Karen turned around and flopped onto the sofa.

Edda could see that the young woman was confused. She sat down next to her. "What's wrong? I thought you had moved on."

"I…" Karen ran her hand across her forehead, "I don't know what I want."

"You have to make your mind up, Karen, before it goes too far."

"Don't you think I know that?" she cried. She slumped forward, resting her head in her hands.

"You love him." It was more a statement than a question, and one that surprised them both.

"I don't know, and I don't want to know."

Edda finally saw the problem. "You're scared. You've finally found someone that you really care about and you're terrified."

"You make it sound so…sinister." Karen gazed at her. "Besides, a long-distance relationship never works."

"How do you know that? You won't know until you try."

"I don't know if I want to try. Why not end it before it begins?"

"Because you could miss out on something wonderful." Edda put her hand on Karen's back and rubbed. "Are you afraid of the commitment?"

"When did you become Dear Abby?" Karen snapped.

"Since you decided to ruin a perfectly good relationship."

"Relationship? I hardly know the man."

"Karen, the last time you saw him you kissed him, gave him your business card and asked him to call you. You can't have it both ways."

"I've changed my mind."

"All right, but you have to do the right thing and tell him."

"Couldn't I just write a note or something?"

"Kaaarrreeen," Edda drawled menacingly, "he deserves better than that, and you know it."

"Yeah, I know."

Edda tried not to laugh at the forlorn look on Karen's face. Her merriment was further improved when she realized she had done what David had offered her right at the beginning of their relationship—become his matchmaker. She only hoped that it all didn't come back to her and bite her in the butt.

†

Edda had to restrain herself from pacing while waiting for David and Karen to return from their picnic. For the hundredth time she questioned her involvement in their business. It would be a challenging courtship with the distance factor alone, but Karen's ambivalence added another layer of difficulty to an already complicated relationship.

She heard a knock on the door and took a moment to compose herself. "Stay calm," she muttered to herself. After all, it wouldn't be appropriate for her to show too much interest in their love life.

Edda opened the door and stepped aside to let them in. Their expressions appeared positive, so maybe Karen had changed her mind…again. "How was the picnic?" she asked nonchalantly.

"Good," David replied. "Great in fact."

"Go through to the kitchen and I'll get us coffee." She followed them to the kitchen, resisting the urge to high-five herself.

David put down the basket and blanket and pulled out a chair for Karen. Once she had been seated he took his place next to her.

Edda bit her lip as she made the coffee. She wanted to know everything, but she also wanted to be told and not have to ask. After she placed the mugs on the table she grabbed the cookie jar.

"So," Edda said.

"So," David repeated, grinning at her.

"So," Karen said, looking a bit dazed.

"Nice day for a picnic."

"Pretty good." David took a sip of his coffee.

Edda couldn't decide whether they knew exactly what she was after or they were just that stupid. The twinkle in David's eye leaned her toward her first option.

When she could stand it no longer she caved in. "Okay, you win. How did it go?"

"Let's just say we've come to an arrangement."

"David!"

"We talked and decided to give ourselves twelve months to see if this could work."

Edda glanced at Karen. "You agreed to this?"

"Yes."

"What about you, David?"

"It's not my ideal outcome, but I understand there will be long-distance problems to contend with."

I hope you do. Edda knew there was nothing more she could say on the subject and remained quiet. Now she only hoped there weren't any Karen-related problems to contend with too.

†

Edda declined the invitation to join them for dinner and was content to have a quiet night in. Besides, she was not going to be a third wheel in that relationship. She sat on the sofa and indulged herself in a bit of reading. When she finally looked up it was nine o'clock. "Jasper?" It was then she realized she hadn't seen her pesky feline all day.

Jasper had taken to prowling the neighborhood and Edda habitually left the back door slightly ajar for him to come in. She had a deadline of ten o'clock before she locked up and if Jasper was still outside then he was on his own. Maybe he'd found a girlfriend. Hmmm…maybe she should check to see if he was neutered before he became the Casanova of the feline world.

Her eyes became heavy and she struggled to read for more than half an hour. What she really wanted was a soft pillow and a warm bed. Unable to keep her eyes open any longer, Edda left a message for Karen to lock up and prayed the girl read it before going to bed. She would wake up in the morning with either a pussycat or a burglarized home.

†

"Good morning." Edda sat at the kitchen table, mug in hand, and watched Karen drag herself into the kitchen. "Good night?"

"Surprisingly good, actually." Karen smiled at her mischievously.

"Errr, I don't want to know."

"Really? I thought you wanted to know everything, especially since you have been poking your nose into my business."

"Someone had to give you a push, and you know it. Sit down."

Karen collapsed into the chair while Edda grabbed another mug of coffee. She fetched the milk and sugar and plopped them down in front of her. "There you go."

"Thanks," Karen mumbled.

"Did you find the message I left?"

"Yeah. That cat of yours didn't turn up."

"It's not like him. I'll give him one more day before I panic."

Karen took several sips of the coffee then stood up and went to the refrigerator. "I'll probably leave in about an hour, unless you have something else in mind." She took out the fruit juice and went to the cupboard for a glass.

"I don't. Have you checked with David?" Edda couldn't keep the smile off her face.

"He's busy. Something about a previous engagement."

"Must be the other girlfriend."

"Don't start!" Karen put the glass on the table then went back to the cupboard for cereal and a bowl. "We both know he isn't seeing someone else."

"How do you know? Did he tell you?"

"He wouldn't be working so hard to keep this one if he was seeing someone else."

"Logical." Edda knew David better than Karen did and knew he wasn't capable of such a despicable act. "As long as you have the box for Barbara you can go whenever you please."

An hour later Karen carried her bag down the stairs to her car. Edda followed behind with the box and handed it over for Karen to pack in the trunk. "When will I be back?" Karen asked.

"That'll depend on Barbara, but maybe three to four weeks. Do you think you'll survive?" A hint of a smile tugged Edda's lips.

"More to the point, will David survive?"

"You *will* return his calls, won't you?"

"Yeessss Mom," Karen said impatiently.

The rev of the engine drew David out of his house and Edda stood by while the two of them mooned over one another. When she'd finally had enough she stepped in.

"David, I believe you have things to do." He reluctantly let Karen go. "And Karen, don't you want to get home?"

"I've got a little time."

"I seem to recall that you wanted some time off?" Edda looked at her sternly.

"But Edda—"

"Don't 'but Edda' me. I'm not going to stand here while you two while away the hours deciding who's going to leave first."

"Come on, Edda."

"Karen, have a safe trip." She pulled the young woman into a brief hug. "Thanks for coming. I'll let you know when the box is ready to come back to me."

"Enjoy your life in the country."

David snickered.

"And you," she addressed David, "I'll catch up with you later." Edda left the two of them standing by Karen's car.

Sometime later David and Karen were still standing by the car, and there seemed to be no indication that either of them were going anywhere any time soon. Edda watched them from the living room window and shook her head. For someone trying to get out of a relationship, Karen was sure making it difficult for herself.

†

A couple of hours later Edda looked out to see Karen's car gone. She was sure the whole street would have seen the spectacle and she laughed. "Serves him right."

At that moment she thought she felt something brush her leg. "About time—" she grumbled. But when she looked down there was nothing there. Jasper was noticeably absent and Edda now started to panic. She checked the house thoroughly, but he was gone.

She spent the next hour cruising the neighborhood in search of Jasper, slowly working her way along the street, calling out in the hope he would respond.

"This will mean some serious time inside, mister!"

What if he was injured or worse, dead? She didn't want to consider that possibility because he was her last link to June. Despite it all, he had been a comfort and, well, she missed him. With all her visits to the hospital recently, maybe he was giving her a taste of her own medicine by not staying at home.

"Jasper. Come on now. Wouldn't you like some milk?" At this point she was not above bribing him.

Edda had nearly reached the limits of the estate and stood in front of the caretaker's house. She was about to give up calling when she heard a faint meow. Not sure whether it was Jasper or not, she responded to its obvious distress. It appeared to be coming from old Tom's house or, more to the point, from under it.

Tom's car was missing and the house appeared to be locked up tight. She looked around to see if she was being watched. When she was satisfied that no one had noticed her, Edda slipped into the front yard and followed the pitiful cries. "Jasper?" The cries intensified, as if reacting to her call. "Where are you?" The meows ended at the wall. Edda knelt down and looked under the house. "What are you doing there? Come on." She held out her hand but Jasper seemed reluctant to move. "I won't make you walk home on your own. I promise." As a last resort she added a smile.

Jasper limped over to her, favoring his right front paw. "What have you done to yourself?" Edda gently pulled him toward her once he was within range. He cried loudly until she lifted him up against her. "What's wrong, huh?" She touched his paw and he pulled it back abruptly. "Sore?" He gazed up at her. Gone was the haughty look of disdain that usually resided there. Instead, there was a weary look of shock and pain.

Edda sat down on the ground and put Jasper in her lap. Ever so gently she turned him over onto his back and examined the sore paw. Sticking out of it was a knot of metal, not unlike the spikes that had littered the road and caused the car accident. In fact…it looked exactly like it.

Carefully she pinched the metal and steadily drew it out from Jasper's paw. She clamped down on his wriggling body, which made Jasper fight all the more. Edda ignored the tiny stabs of pain as Jasper dug in his claws to get some purchase to make a run for it. She persevered until the spike had been removed. Jasper's pad was red and inflamed and in need of treatment from a vet. In the meantime she would take him home and do what she could.

She stood with the cat in her arms and heard the sound of a car engine. "Oh shit!" she whispered. It was an innocent rescue but somehow she felt guilty. Maybe she could hide until Tom was safely inside then make her escape. At that moment, Jasper complained loudly. "Shut up! He'll catch us!" she snapped quietly. Jasper just wouldn't listen. It seemed he had decided he'd had enough and wanted to be left alone. Common sense told her to give Jasper what he wanted, but she knew if she did he'd probably crawl away and she'd never see him again. He needed help…and soon.

"Too late." The male voice sounded calm, almost too calm.

"Errr, hi!" she said brightly.

"What's so interesting under my house?"

"My friend here is injured and I'm trying to help him. I heard him crying out while I was on my walk." *So far the truth*.

"What's the matter with him?"

"He trod on something sharp and it got stuck in his paw." Edda showed him the spike. "I think I've seen this before. Do you remember the car accident?"

"I sure do."

"Strange," she muttered absently. "What would this be doing under your house?"

"Maybe the cat picked it up somewhere else and crawled under the house for safety. Did you ever think of that?"

Edda looked up at the hint of annoyance in his voice.

"Sorry. I'll take him to the vet." But she wasn't so sure about Jasper dragging it under the house. He could barely walk to her when she called, so she couldn't see him staggering from the roadway to the house. No, something wasn't right but she couldn't put her finger on it.

"Come inside. I'll see if I have something to wrap around his paw."

"That's very kind of you." Edda followed Tom inside. The décor was not what she expected. "Nice place."

"It's livable," he grumbled.

His house was more than livable, Edda thought. It was downright opulent. He left her waiting in the living room where a massive television screen adorned one wall, with a column speaker sitting in each corner. A recliner chair sat squarely in front of the entertainment center. A bowl of half-eaten popcorn sat next to the chair on a small table. Knickknacks were scattered around the room, some of which looked expensive. If she had to guess Tom had purchased them recently, possibly in the last two to three years; certainly not ten years ago when he bought the house.

Her gaze swept around the room. Where did he get the money? She had been under the impression that he didn't work, having seen him lounging on the front porch on her walks. Was it possible he had come into money with the death of a relative? Unless he revealed the information she would never know, and she knew he was the sort of person who wouldn't give personal information willingly.

"Here."

Edda jumped. She had been so deep in thought that she didn't hear him return.

"Thanks." She sat down on a nearby sofa and put Jasper on her lap. He barely fought her as she wrapped the strip of cloth around his paw. She could see he was tired and probably in shock. "Do you know where the closest vet is?"

"Only one I know of is at the mall. You may have to call ahead, being Sunday and all."

Edda gently lifted Jasper into her arms and pressed him against her chest as she struggled to get off the sofa. "Well, thanks for your kindness."

"No problem." He all but pushed her out the door before closing it behind her.

"Strange man," she muttered. "Come on. Let's get you to the vet."

Twenty minutes later she parked her car in the parking lot. Jasper was very quiet...too quiet. A spike of fear ran through her and she grabbed him and walked quickly to the mall. She found the information board and searched for someone who sounded like a vet. "38C," she said to Jasper. "Let's try Dr. Stillwell." The office's entrance was probably on the outside of the building, so she began her search there. After ten minutes she found it.

Edda called the emergency number on the door and half an hour later the vet and his assistant turned up. "Come on in." He unlocked the door and pushed it aside.

As soon as the door opened there was a cacophony of sound from dogs and birds, all clamoring for attention. She was in the right place.

The waiting room was empty but that didn't stop her looking for a seat. She felt like an idiot. She had every seat to choose from and yet she still looked. Jasper squirmed in her arms. It was a good sign from him and Edda was pressed to keep a hold on him.

The girl stopped in front of her. "Can you fill this form in?"

Edda gave her an exasperated look. "Sorry, I left my third hand at home."

"Heh, funny." She put down the clipboard with the form on the seat next to her and disappeared into the back room.

Edda looked at the questionnaire. Without physically putting down the cat, she had no hope of even printing her name. It would have to wait.

Ten minutes later, she was escorted into the surgery. She placed Jasper on the table.

"Now what seems to be the problem?"

She so wanted to smack the man upside the head. Wasn't it obvious what the problem was? "He trod on a spike of metal and it cut into the pad of his paw."

The vet unwrapped the bandage and took a look at the damage. "A spike?"

Edda rummaged around in her bag and found the piece of metal. She took it out and showed him.

"That's nasty." He took the metal from her. "Is that off barbed wire fencing?"

"That's what I thought."

"Who would do a thing like that?" He handed the spike back to her.

"These were all over the road near my house. Maybe Jasper picked it up from there."

"Jasper?"

"The cat."

"I don't understand why someone would make these. Not unless they wanted to cause an accident or cripple someone."

"These were found near a car accident. It blew out their tires."

"Well, the spikes would certainly work if you were trying to kill somebody."

He wasn't the first person to say that. It seemed everybody assumed the spikes were on the road for a nefarious purpose rather than an innocent spillage of cargo. The fact that somebody had to make them indicated some form of malice.

Jasper squirmed violently as the vet prodded the wound. His claws lashed out at anyone close enough to get caught. Edda stood back and watched as the vet tried to calm him.

"It's going to need a couple of stitches."

Edda had expected that. It was a nasty gash. "What happens now?"

"We'll give him a light anesthetic." The vet was already in motion as he spoke. "Sandra? I need a hand here."

The young girl appeared, the cheerful smile still plastered on her face.

"Give us about half an hour."

Edda was ushered out the room before she even had the chance to say anything. Jasper's piteous cries nearly had her ready to knock down the door. He wasn't happy and neither was she. "Hang in there, buddy."

She found the form and took a seat on a nearby bench outside. With time to waste, Edda began to fill out the sheet. By the time she completed it there was only ten minutes left, so she remained where she was.

An hour later, and her pocketbook considerably lighter from the bill, Edda finally pulled into the driveway of her home. Jasper lay dozing, slowly recovering from the aftereffects of anesthesia. Edda was pleased that at least he wasn't scratching up the backseat.

She carried Jasper from the car and deposited him gently on the sofa. In an effort to make him more comfortable, Edda pulled an old blanket out of the trunk and made a small nest of it for him to cuddle into. He wasn't going anywhere in a hurry.

Her body cried out for a coffee and she indulged her need. As she sipped it the vet's words came to mind… "The spikes would certainly work if you were trying to kill somebody." Kill somebody. Even though she had already gone through the possibilities after the accident, the vet's words stirred something in her. Was the accident meant for the woman driving the car or for her?

Edda refilled her cup as she thought about the possibility that someone out there was trying to kill her. Who would want to do that and, more importantly, why? As far as she was aware there had only been the one attempt, and that attempt had not been proven to be just that. Was she making more out of this than it actually was?

No. The criminals had been caught and the police were satisfied the case had been solved. She had to let it go. Jasper had simply trod on an errant spike.

Chapter Nineteen

Edda slept soundly, deep enough not to hear the muted footsteps of someone climbing the stairs. The intruder walked slowly and silently into her bedroom and looked down at her sleeping form. Before she could wrench herself out of sleep, a chloroform-soaked cloth was placed over her nose and mouth and held there until her body went limp. Edda was in deep, deep trouble and she didn't even know it.

†

The first moment of consciousness was disorienting. The most obvious sensation was an excruciating pain in her side, one that she didn't remember being inflicted with. She shifted gently and felt like she was lying on a bed of nails, with tiny pinpoints of white-hot agony skittering over her back and legs.

Edda opened her eyes and saw a man standing over her with a shovel, his menacing glare pinning her in place. "Help me." Vainly she held up a hand, but she knew she wouldn't

213

be getting help from him. The movement exacerbated her pain and she moved her hand to her side to feel something had pierced her side and was still embedded there.

"Why?"

"You had to keep digging around," he said as he lowered himself into the pit she had been dropped in. "Now you'll take that information to your grave." He chuckled at his own sick joke.

"I don't understand. I don't know any information." Her gaze took in her surroundings and she realized the seriousness of her own predicament. She had been thrown into the coffin she herself had dug up weeks ago. Her hand again went to her side and felt the object sticking into her. It was round and smooth. It was a bone. She slowly turned her head to find herself nose to nose with a skull.

Her body jumped and she instantly regretted it. Edda dropped her head back and tried to breathe slowly. Her heart was beating at a blistering pace as she contemplated what the next few minutes would hold for her.

"Any last words?" The man sneering at her wasn't the same man she had talked to on her walks around the estate. Tom the caretaker was Tom the killer.

"It was you? Why?"

He looked around the surrounding land, as if looking for any signs of rescue. His gaze returned to her eyes. "I don't suppose it matters. He started pokin' around the coffins that were bein' moved 'ere. I could see 'im clear as day, so I snuck up on 'im and caught 'im pulling out cash. It was all so simple really. He'd left a shovel nearby. One smack over the 'ead and bury him in the coffin he had dug up. Sweet like."

Edda smacked her lips. It seemed shock was setting in and there was nothing she could do about it. At least if she fainted she was already lying down. Death had a wicked sense of humor.

"Why now?"

"Now? Them others were being released from prison. I knew they'd come a-lookin'. Wanted 'em to think he'd taken the money and run."

"Why me? The case is closed. I was no danger to you." The pain was overwhelming her but it was the last piece of the puzzle that she needed to know.

"The barb wire."

"What about it? The cat got it into its paw. I thought it was an accident…ah, but you didn't. You thought I had figured it out. That's ironic."

"Iron-what?"

"You thought I was poking around, but in fact I was just rescuing my cat from under your house. This would have been unnecessary."

"Now it is. It's too late."

Edda screamed like her life depended on it. She only managed one scream before Tom struck out with his shovel. She fended it off as best she could and her arms took the brunt of his rage, all the while yelling for help. He finally stopped and glared down at her. Quickly, he pulled the lid into the hole and placed it over the coffin. Edda beat against the wood as he secured the screws, knowing this was her last few moments of fresh air. Tom had won after all, although ironically, it was a death that could have easily been avoided.

Her fists slammed against the braced wood ineffectually. Soil being shoveled on top of her dampened the resonance of the wood and her hopes of rescue faded. With each shovel of soil, she felt the weight of it on her soul. She had reached the end of the line.

Edda stopped pounding. It was dark and claustrophobic, and her mind filled with despair. Despite all her attempts to get on with her life, it appeared she would be joining June after all. "I won't be long, love," she whispered before she closed her eyes.

Time was irrelevant in her small space. The pain from the bones underneath her back had moved to intense irritation. She was so sick of being in pain, being impotent about saving herself and sick of all the high drama surrounding the cemetery. She had her fill of crime-solving and longed for the ease of a normal life. Of course, that possibility was now gone and she would fade from people's memories with a whimper. She would disappear without a trace.

Her fist rose to the lid and she thought about continuing her resistance. Was there any point? After all, no one would hear her knocks or calls, but giving up was accepting her death.

What about David? Or even Delia? She had just started to enjoy her time with them and now it had been cut short. What would she say to them if she had one last chance? David had been a godsend, saving not only her life but her sanity on a number of occasions. She was honored to call him friend.

Delia was another story. From a chance meeting in the hospital, Delia had proven to be someone she wished she had gotten to know better. Someone she felt she could have grown closer to. Someone she could have cared about…a lot. She closed her eyes and allowed her mind to drift. It seemed the Fates had decided that she could have no life other than the one she had shared with June. Now it was time to move on.

†

Edda had no idea how long she had been in the coffin. In fact, she had no idea whether the sun was up or if it was still dark. Was it hours or only mere minutes? She breathed shallowly to try and conserve the air left to her. It was then that she heard a voice calling to her. Her oxygen-depleted mind leapt to the conclusion that she was on the other side. "June? I'm here honey."

"Edda?" She heard it again. She banged on the coffin lid and yelled, "June! I'm here." It took her a few moments to understand that the voice was male.

"Edda, we're coming to get you." The words were soft but distinct.

"Here!" she yelled. It was an inane thing to say, but common sense was not a high priority.

It was several minutes before she heard another noise. It persisted for a while longer and grew steadily louder until something hit the coffin lid with a bang. She could only assume that it was a shovel, and she fervently hoped that it was indeed her rescue party.

"Edda? Are you in there?"

"Yeah," she hollered. Weariness and pain weighed heavily on her and she was glad the ordeal was nearly over. Her body had suffered a lot during her move and if it wasn't for the fact that Tom had now been revealed she would seriously consider going home. Now it was only a matter of time before he would be put away and out of her hair. The thought added promise to smooth sailing from now on in her life.

Edda waited impatiently to be free of her prison, and she kept her rising panic in check. The lid finally came away and she looked up at the face of her savior. It didn't really surprise her it was David.

David grinned down at her. "Hey, stranger. Can I give you a lift?" A momentary frown crossed his face as he took in the state of her arms. "What happened?" he said angrily.

"I had another run-in with a shovel. They're out to get me, I tell you." Edda smiled weakly. He lowered his hand and Edda reached for it. Pain shot through her back and side, reminding her of the bones she had been lying on. "Can't." She gasped in reaction to her jostling.

David tilted his head up. "Hey! I could use a hand here!" More faces appeared above her, including Detective Webber. "Detective Wi…Wen…" she uttered.

"Webber," David and the detective answered in unison.

"Did you get him?"

"He's in custody. Lucky for you we had him under surveillance. I couldn't have even begun to figure out where he had hidden you if we hadn't." Webber looked up and called out, "We need to get this coffin out."

David lowered himself to the ground and lay there to keep Edda company. "Just rest and we'll have you out of there in no time."

Edda looked at David. "How did you know? Were you spying on me again?"

"Actually, I was having a smoke outside and I saw that guy carrying something over his shoulder out to the cemetery. I called the cops and we met at the path. I wondered how they'd gotten there so quickly."

Edda breathed steadily. It suddenly hit her that she had nearly died and her body shuddered. If the police hadn't been on hand it would have become a reality, and she was not sure she was ready for that. She liked the life she had found, and while June would always be in her heart and in her memories, it was time to pick up the strands of her existence and step forward.

"You okay?"

"Y-Y-yeah." Edda lifted a hand and saw it was shaking. "Don't tell Delia, all right?"

"Really?" David's eyes twinkled mischievously.

"Just…don't." She had neither the energy nor the calmness to discuss what he thought about Delia. The bones shifted underneath her and she moved. "I…think…I…can…" Slowly and steadily she lifted her upper body up. The pieces fell away from her clothing and clattered back to the skeleton. "Oww." The piece in her side dislodged, leaving behind a dull ache.

"Here." David's hand appeared above her and she took it. He steadily pulled her up until she was standing.

Edda ached all over. It was a bone-deep ache that she could barely tolerate. Another hand appeared and she grabbed it. Between the two men they hoisted her out of the hole and onto firm ground. She gingerly threw her arms around David and held on for dear life. "I have never been so happy to see you." He tightened his hold on her and her composure failed her. Tears cascaded down her cheeks and dampened David's shirt.

"It's okay," he whispered in her ear. "You're safe now." His hand rubbed up and down her back slowly.

Edda nodded in agreement as the tears increased. Death had come calling but left without her. *Sorry, June.* While her reunion with her lover was delayed, she knew inevitably that they would meet again. In the meantime, she had a life to resume.

"Miss Case."

"Detective We…Webber. Nice to be standing up."

He laughed. "That's a bit of an understatement. The EMTs will be here soon."

"I don't need—"

"Please don't embarrass me by not accepting their treatment. We can all see that you're a little banged up."

While the bruises on her arms would fade in time, the hole in her side was of more concern, and she knew that it would be prudent to see a doctor about it. Who knew what germs loitered in the bones she had been lying on. As her mother used to say, "it's better to be safe than sorry," but she suspected that she would be both safe and very sorry.

"What happened?"

"I found my cat injured underneath his house. He thought I was spying on him."

David sighed before he spoke. "Why am I not surprised?"

"No, really. Poor Jasper had one of those metal knots in his foot. If you don't believe me, he's resting on the sofa."

David held up his hands. "No! No, I believe you, but obviously Tom didn't."

"Which is strange because he got me a bandage for Jasper's foot."

"Maybe he thought you had put two and two together."

"Maybe. At any rate he wanted to make sure I didn't tell anyone else."

Detective Webber spoke up, "I hope you learned from this adventure, Miss Case. Poking your nose into police business is very dangerous, possibly fatal."

"I've learned my lesson, Detective." Edda caught David's wry expression in her peripheral vision. "I can't afford all the medical bills."

An ambulance siren announced the arrival of the EMTs. Detective Webber left David and Edda alone while he walked down the incline to the assembled officers waiting for instructions.

The two paramedics trotted up to her. "What seems to be the problem?"

David quickly apprised them of the situation and Edda added her own comments about what happened. While the injuries were not life-threatening, Edda couldn't avoid another trip to the hospital. On the way one of the EMTs even joked about putting her address on speed dial.

She was escorted into the ER and immediately recognized.

"Back again, Miss Case?"

Edda didn't know the nurse in question but she didn't dispute it. The last two times she was admitted she was unconscious. "Yeah. I'm thinking of getting a guide dog."

The nurse laughed. "Probably not a bad idea. I'll get Nurse Parsons for you."

"Who's Nurse Parsons?" Edda couldn't recall that name.

"Delia."

"Oh no, no, no. The woman thinks I'm a klutz as it is. Please don't confirm it."

"All right. I'll see if I can bump you up the line as you're one of our best customers."

"Oh, Lord," Edda grumbled as she sank down in her seat in the waiting room. Apart from the various pains in her body she now had a large dose of embarrassment to deal with.

Three hours later Edda found David asleep in the waiting room. He stirred when she nudged him. "Ready to go home?"

"Yeah, finally." She was tired and sore and in dire need of a coffee.

"What did the doctor say?"

"Nothing major. A couple of stitches in my side and a tetanus shot. I need to come back in a couple of days for a check-up."

He guided her to his car and helped her into the passenger seat. "Is this the end of it?" David asked seriously.

"Yeah, it is." Edda looked out the window as David closed the door and climbed behind the steering wheel. "It's done."

Chapter Twenty

By the time Edda walked in her front door, she had just about had all the prodding she could take for one day. It was midafternoon, but the way she felt it could have been midnight. All she wanted to do was to find a coffee and then a bed.

David was about to leave, his job of taxi driver done.

"David? Would you like a coffee?" Edda tried to hide her exhaustion from him but she suspected she wasn't successful.

"I don't think—"

"Please, I'm not quite ready to be alone." The doctor had stitched up the hole in her side and now the local anesthetic was beginning to wear off. She couldn't decide which hurt worse, her side or her arm, which throbbed from the tetanus shot.

David's lips tilted upward.

"What?"

"I can remember a time when that was all you wanted."

"It seems like a lifetime ago." In a way it was. It was a time of transition. Her crossroads.

"Sit down. I can get this."

She took a seat and watched him move around her kitchen competently. A ball of fur bounced up and landed in her lap, scaring the life out of her. "Whaaa…? Oh Geezus, Jasper. Are you trying to kill me?" She was already in pain. Now Jasper made her twitch and stretch her abused and stitched muscles.

"You okay?" David called over his shoulder.

"Yeah. Damned cat." But that didn't stop Edda from stroking the soft fur.

David put down the mug in front of a waiting Edda. She inhaled deeply to absorb the aroma.

"You don't have to snort it."

"Coffee. There's nothing like it."

"Well, maybe cigarettes, cocaine, and marijuana. The list goes on."

She clicked her tongue at him. "Coffee is my addiction of choice."

"I know." He gazed at her over the top of his mug. "So, now that everything is tied up nicely with a bright bow, what are you going to do?"

"Do?"

David looked into his mug. "I suppose I was wondering whether you were going to stick around now that the mystery has been solved." He didn't look her in the eye and she suspected he was afraid to hear the answer.

"Well, I haven't talked to Lesley yet, so I suppose it will depend on her."

"If you want my opinion—"

"As if I could stop you."

"—my opinion, please stay."

"I thought I was the most exasperating female on the planet."

"Who I adore," he said quietly.

Edda leaned over the table and grabbed his hand. "You're not so bad yourself."

They looked at each other for a moment before David stood and placed their mugs in the sink. "Well, I'll let you get some rest. If there's anything you need…"

"I've got your number."

"Right then." He made his way through her house to the front door. "Later!" he called. She heard the front door close and she was alone. Jasper lay content on her lap, snoring gently while dreaming his feline-tainted dreams. She knew she had put off the decision for some time now, and it was time to commit.

Edda shifted Jasper to the sofa before fetching her cell. She found Lesley's number and waited for her to answer. "Lesley? Hi, it's Edda. I think it's probably time to discuss the house swap…"

†

Edda waited a few days before contacting Delia. She wanted to make sure that she could hide the scrapes and bruises from Delia before she saw her, because the woman would not let her forget it otherwise. She dialed the familiar number and waited for the call to be answered.

"Hello?"

"Delia? It's Edda."

"What's wrong?"

"Why should there be anything wrong?"

"C'mon, Edda. Every time I hear from you something's happened. What is it this time?"

"Actually, I was going to ask you over for dinner."

225

"Really?"

"Really. I'm feeling a little down and could use the company of a friend." The silence on the other end of the phone didn't bode well. Was Delia still holding a grudge? She thought they had gotten past that, and while tempted to question her about it, Edda decided to keep her mouth shut. She seemed to have the unnerving habit of putting her foot in it.

"What time?"

"Seven good for you?"

"Sure. Where?"

"My place. Don't bring a thing—except yourself of course."

"See you then."

The call ended before Edda could say goodbye. Something was definitely bugging Delia and she was determined she would find out what it was. Edda turned her attention to what she was going to serve her recalcitrant guest.

†

The doorbell rang and Edda straightened her blouse. She had taken some effort with her appearance this time and she wasn't sure why. Her initial plan had been to cover up the aftereffects of her scrape with death, which she had achieved successfully with a long-sleeve blouse. Of course the blouse only went with one pair of pants, which led to low heels and a touch of perfume. Suddenly she felt like she was going out on a date.

Edda opened the door and welcomed her guest. "Hey. Nice to see you. Come in." She stepped aside to let Delia in. "Let me take that." She grabbed Delia's coat and hung it up on the hat stand while Delia put her handbag down on the small table sitting next to it. Delia stared at her.

"What?" Edda looked to where her gaze lay. "Oh."

"You said you were feeling down. It certainly doesn't look like it."

"Would you have come otherwise?" Edda asked. "But yesterday I was feeling sorry for myself. Today is another day."

Delia relaxed, apparently satisfied with the explanation. Edda walked off, half-expecting Delia to follow her. When she didn't she walked back to the front door. "Are you coming?"

"Is there any point to this?"

"You don't think salvaging our friendship is worth the effort? I'm heartbroken."

"I'm being serious here." Delia stood there, refusing to move.

"I'm trying to be, but you're making it awfully hard to do so." Edda held out her hand. "Come on."

Delia looked at her hand as if it were radioactive. When it wasn't taken, Edda moved on. She took a seat on the sofa, patting the space next to her. "Sit down." With a deep sigh, Delia did as she was asked.

"What's the problem?" Edda said gently. "I thought we were good friends."

"There's no problem. We're friends. Let's just leave it at that."

"Then there's no problem. Right?" Edda looked hopefully at her friend.

"No, no problem." But Delia's voice had a sound of resignation about it.

Edda reached across and laid her hand on top of Delia's. "Please don't do that," Delia muttered.

"Oh." She had thought her sexuality hadn't been a problem for Delia. Apparently it was. "I'm sorry. I wasn't coming on to you."

"I figured that," Delia said in a monotone. Something was definitely up.

Something mentally clicked in her brain and Edda knew what the problem was. "Did you want me to?" Delia blushed…badly. "I didn't think—"

"No, you didn't."

"Well." What could she say? "Look—"

"I don't need an explanation. I know what you're going to say." Delia fidgeted and stood abruptly. "This was a bad idea."

"Talk to me, Dee. What's going on with you?" Edda stood as well and tried to close the distance between them.

"Never mind." Delia moved away and walked toward the front door.

"What do you want to know?" Edda blurted out. She now had her suspicions but she was scared that if they were wrong she could destroy her friendship once and for all. "Let's get this out in the open so we both know where we stand."

Delia stood facing the front door, her back ramrod-straight. Seconds passed before she turned and looked at her. Edda could see the indecision in her eyes and waited patiently while Delia processed her words. "Come on. Sit down," she murmured. Edda didn't wait this time, instead taking a seat on the single chair next to the sofa. "Spill it."

Delia sat on the sofa like she was sitting on a bed of nails, squirming restlessly on the seat. Edda kept focused on her.

"Do I have a chance?"

Delia had spoken so quietly Edda barely heard it. Surprisingly, Jasper walked up to the sofa and jumped onto

Delia's lap without so much as a hiss. Delia held her hands out from her body. "What's he doing?"

"I have no idea. Jasper?" The cat glanced at her then settled down where he was. A gentle purr could be heard in the ensuing silence. "Errr. He likes you?"

"Did you drug him or something?"

"Not that I know of, but it sure seems he's had a change of heart. Try patting him."

"Are you crazy? He'll probably chew my hands off." At Edda's urging, Delia slowly reached out and placed her hand on Jasper's back. When he didn't object she slowly stroked him. The purr picked up speed until it sounded like a small motor.

Edda stared at the cat. The sudden change of attitude seemed strange, and yet maybe not. Was this June's way of telling her to get on with her life? The question was…could she?

"Do I have a chance?" Delia repeated.

Edda leaned back in her seat and gazed at the ceiling for a moment before she answered. "Yes, but it's complicated." The gobsmacked look on Delia's face brought a smile to her lips. "Didn't expect that, huh? Neither did I."

"So…" Delia swallowed noisily. "So where do we go from here?"

"I don't know if I'm ready for that next step yet. It's only been three months since June's death."

"I'm sorry I—"

"Don't be. It's not your fault. It's me. I'm conflicted enough over returning to work this early. I guess I'm still coming to terms with everything. Can we still be friends for now? You'll be the first to know when I'm ready."

Edda watched Delia carefully as she mulled over the offer. Maybe it wasn't what she was exactly looking for, but it was how it needed to be.

"I don't have much choice, do I?"

"There are always choices—not good ones but choices nonetheless." Edda frowned as she tried to sort out what she wanted to say. "It's not a life sentence, Delia. All I'm asking for is a little time to put everything into perspective. You are an amazing woman and I would like to get to know you better, if you'll allow me."

"I'm not amazing." Delia's cheeks turned red.

"You are. More than you know. You saved me."

"I'm a nurse."

"Not that kind of save. You were there when I needed a shoulder to cry on, when I needed company with no expectations. That is special, Dee. To be able to anticipate what I need and be there."

"Oh, hush." The rose hue spread over her face and neck.

"I talked to Lesley a couple of days ago." Edda waited for Delia to say something but she didn't. "The position she'd been in temporarily has now become a permanent one. I'm staying here."

"What about the house?"

"For now, we'll pay the utilities ourselves and arrange shipment of our things. I suppose I better think about getting the address changed on my license." Delia couldn't suppress her smile.

Edda then uttered the words she knew Delia was so desperate to hear. "So let's go forward from here and see where our future leads us."

She felt comfortable with her decision. Jasper looked over at her and winked. It seemed that June had been watching over her after all.

THE END

About the Author

Name

Erica Lawson

Erica Lawson is a "dinky di" Aussie, born and raised in Sydney, Australia. She has worked as a secretary for most of her working life in a variety of interesting fields from a government scientific organization, the fire brigade, the film industry and finally, for the last twenty years, with a psychiatrist. Many of her friends will attest to the fact that she finally found her niche in the last job, gaining many helpful hints for her own state of mind.

Her first book, *Possessing Morgan*, was released in December 2009. It is a winner of the 2010 GCLS award for best thriller/mystery novel. Her second book *The Chronicles of Ratha: The Children Of The Noorthi*, a science fiction adventure, was released in December 2010 and was a finalist in the 2012 GCLS Awards. Erica's third novel, *Soulwalker*, released in 2012, won both the Rainbow Award for Best Sci-Fi of 2012 and GCLS Best Speculative Fiction in 2013. Her fourth novel, *Reflected Passion* won Best Historical Fiction at GCLS in 2014.

Erica has three novels published with Affinity eBooks. *Miss-Match*, co-written with A.C. Henley, in April 2013. Her first solo effort for Affinity, *Out Of Retirement*, came out in April 2014. Finally, her third novel, a sequel to *The Chronicles of Ratha*, called *A Lion Among The Lambs* was released in December 2014.

Erica now writes solely for Affinity eBooks and her previous novels, first released through Blue Feather Books, are being reissued by Affinity. They are available through Affinity eBooks website, Amazon, Barnes and Noble, and Bella Books.

Erica Lawson also writes under the name "Aurelia" on online fan fiction. Her website link is: http://www.ericalawson.com and her Yahoo group is Aurelia's Musings.

Other Books from Affinity eBook Press

Locked Inside—Annette Mori   One day Belinda is a normal rambunctious ten year old until a mysterious illness attacks her body rendering her completely immobile, mute, and unaware of her surroundings for six years. Her last thought before slipping into a coma was I don't want to die. Awareness comes slowly to Belinda after six years after she hears a couple of giggling girls. Belinda panics when she realizes that her body and voice will not cooperate s Coppice Formatwith the signals her brain is sending. She is unable to capture the attention of those around her to let them know that there is a person locked inside. Fortunately for Belinda, one of the teenagers is Carly, a beautiful and vivacious young woman who recognizes the person locked inside. Carly and Belinda form an unusual bond of friendship. Will Carly's love help Belinda break free from her prison and will their relationship evolve into something much greater friendship. How much does the power of love matter to someone who must overcome obstacles far greater than most people face in a lifetime.

Line of Sight—Ali Spooner   Sasha and her lover Kara are back. This time on the trail of a killer in the city of New Orleans. They sense his presence as he prowls the French Quarter committing the murders, but fail to find him. Abandoned by his domineering lover, a killer wreaks havoc on the city. His narcissistic behavior fuels his need to terminate his sexual partners, believing his consumption of their power will bring his beloved back to him. When the killer sets his sights on young Milly, will Sasha's psychic connection with her aid in Milly's rescue, and perpetuate the capture of the killer? Continue the thrilling adventures of this couple from the Sasha Thibodaux series.

Loving Again—Alicia Joseph Dana Perkins lost her longtime partner in a tragic accident. Although she still struggles with the loss, her profound loneliness is evidence that it is time to move on. She knows her deceased lover, Casey, wouldn't want her living this way. Dana begins her slow process of letting go, removing reminders of Casey from her house, and dating again. The women she meets, leave Dana uninspired and missing her deceased partner even more. Just as she is about to resign herself to the belief that she will never love again, Dana meets Emily Daniels, a married woman who is deeply conflicted over her attraction to women. Soon, the two women form a friendship that leads to deeper emotions. They discover that one moment in their past had brought them together in a way neither woman could have ever imagined. Is that one moment in time enough to let both women follow their hearts, or will they let their past continue to rule their future?

Against All Odds—JM Dragon.. From award winning and bestselling author JM Dragon, with significant updates by, Erin O'Reilly comes an original tale of romance where everything seems to be stacked against two women whose destinies bring them together. Stephanie Grant has a past that she can never escape. Attempting a fresh start, she opens an art gallery in the small town of Mapleton hoping that her wondering spirit will allow her to stay. A chance encounter with vivacious Louise Masterson has Steph thinking in the long-term for the first time in her life. Louise, a high school teacher and the daughter of the richest man in town, has a stubborn streak. She refuses to knuckle down to her domineering father's demands and lives a simple life away from the family home. After meeting Stephanie Grant, her world changes and love looms on the horizon. Life however takes a twisted path setting both Steph and Louise in directions they never thought possible. Will love win out against all odds or will love be forever lost?

The Settlement—Ali Spooner Crushed when her lover Missy, a social worker, dies from an error made during an operation, Cadin Michaels vows to make the guilty pay for their deadly error. Settling out of court, and receiving a handsome award, does nothing to ease Cadin's grief, and her law partner encourages her to take a sabbatical to "find herself again." She uses the settlement to create a foundation in Missy's name to continue her work with women and children. Cadin mounts her motorcycle and lets fate lead her on a soul-cleansing adventure. She encounters people on her adventures who refresh her belief in kindness, and unconditional love. She forms a plan to use the funds from Missy's Foundation to give others a fresh start in life. Realizing she too needs a fresh start, Cadin finds herself drawn to the chemistry she feels for a woman she encounters in Alabama. The outpouring of love and friendship helps her on her path to healing and learning to trust her heart to love once again.

Once Upon a Time—Alane Hotchkin Many centuries ago, a vision came to the royal seer with a prophecy that showed a warlord ruling the land until she came to claim what was rightfully hers. Princess Kataryna's widowed father, King Theos, raised her from birth, to one day, become queen and rule over Pavlone. When she turned fifteen the princess had no idea that the Fates would start her on an obscure path to her final destiny. On that day as she rode into a meadow of wildflowers a dark rider came upon her, thus beginning her tumultuous journey of love and adventure. Raven only wanted to escape the blows that life had dealt her. She longed to be on the open sea and free. When she came upon a beautiful young girl sitting alone in the middle of a meadow, little did she know that her destiny would be changed forever. Will they become the pawns of the ancient vision or will both paths lead to the same port of destiny? Find out it in this exciting high seas adventure that will capture your imagination.

Asset Management—Annette Mori Toni, Sophie, and Kim, are the modern day version of Robin Hood blended with the Three Musketeers. For the past eighteen months, they have been moving the assets of the rapacious bank executives to the more deserving coffers—at least in their minds—of the poor and middle class. When a mysterious woman keeps crossing paths with Toni, sparks fly. Is it a coincidence or all part of some greater master plan? Is she friend or foe? Add the Russian mob, the FBI, and an all-female covert organization and you have the perfect recipe for danger, intrigue, and even love. Does the trio join forces with the organization? Follow the twists and turns to the explosive conclusion. Not everything is black and white. There are many shades of gray and sometimes it's difficult to decipher who is good and who is evil. No one is all virtue or all malevolence, but sometimes love helps us rise above.

Do Dreams Come True?—JM Dragon Laurel Rogers was unceremoniously dumped by her long-time lover, painter Ronnie Lancaster, finding her belongings outside the apartment they shared. To add to her misery, the next day she loses her job, fired by the Dragon of Finance, Christen Jamison. What else can go wrong? Oh yes, her best friend becomes engaged to the brother of the Dragon. For ten years, Christen Jamison has never forgiven her partner for walking out on her. She's given up on love, making her work her life as the accountant for the family business. After she is directed to fire a woman who should never have been on the redundancy list—Laurel Rogers—Christen begins to doubt her commitment to the store's management and policies. How do two people who really shouldn't get on end up in a relationship? Find out in this deliciously ordinary romance.

Return to Me—Erin O'Reilly Renowned microbiologist Sydney Tanner left work as normal for her trip home but never arrived. Ellie Scott her wife of ten years frantically, to the point of obsession, attempts to find her—the only evidence there is something amiss is Syd's crashed truck, then the clues go cold. Ellie refuses to believe that she will never see Syd again but realizes many months later with nothing solid to go on, it's time to attempt to move forward with a life without Syd. Leaving her home town she accepts a new job at Salvation, aptly named for Ellie's predicament. There Ellie meets beautiful Maya Rojas who is the director of Salvation—a rehabilitation hospital. Although she hasn't given up on finding Syd, Ellie finds herself increasingly drawn to Maya. Will Salvation bring just that to Ellie, allowing her to find peace and happiness again, or will it have her questioning all that she believes in? A wonderful romance cloaked within an intriguing mystery.

Terminal Event—Ali Spooner Tally Rainwater was born with the gift of second sight, something she never understood. A near-fatal accident, at age twelve, makes her visions clearer, but not the reason for them. As she matures, Lisa, a spirit, enters her visions to guide her in using her gift, but still not the reason why. After Tally's gift helps locate the body of a murdered teen, she realizes her gift is to help lost souls find their peace. When it's discovered, a serial killer murdered the teen, Blair "Spooky" Cooper is the Agent in Charge assigned to the case. A task force of local detectives and FBI forms to track the killer. Blair enlists the aid of Tally, and together with the team, Tally helps them piece together the puzzle of murders spanning twenty years throughout the Deep South. Even with the complication of the case, Blair and Tally have an undeniable attraction to each other. As they close in on the killer, the killer focuses on Tally, jeopardizing her bond with Blair and everyone around her. For the sake of the case, they put their attraction on the back burner until the killer is caught. Will the killer be caught or continue to evade authorities? Can Tally and Blair's budding romance survive the possibility? Read this intense murder mystery romance and find out.

Arc Over Time—Jen Silver Dr Kathryn Moss has job offers flowing in after her exciting archaeological discoveries at Starling Hill the previous year. Now she has choices to make that could jeopardise her relationship with Denise Sullivan, the fiery journalist, who has become her lover. For Denise the choice seems obvious. She thinks they have moved beyond the casual sex stage to something more like a true relationship. However, she's not sure how to handle Kathryn's continuing infatuation with Ellie Winters. Ellie's new career as a promising artist proves to be a catalyst for the simmering tensions in relations between her wife Robin,

Kathryn, and Denise. Will Denise persevere in her pursuit of the reluctant professor? Does Ellie have anything to fear from Kathryn's fascination with her art, or is there another motive behind the professor's obsessive interest? This wonderful romantic continuation with the characters from Starting Over ties up loose ends. But the question is—does everyone have a happy ending? A must read.

The Presence—Charlene Neal After catching her husband red-handed in bed with his secretary, Kayleigh Gibbs takes her daughter and her Jeep and flees across the country. She opens up her own veterinarian practice, and they move into an old, secluded farmhouse in Hoekwil, South Africa. At her best friend's housewarming party Kayleigh meets the beautiful and enchanting Rebecca Steward. Rebecca is instantly drawn to Kayleigh, but is still recovering from a breakup—her girlfriend left her for a man. She's afraid of a repeat performance with Kayleigh, and won't pursue a romantic relationship with her, preferring instead to develop a platonic friendship. When odd, inexplicable things start happening on the farmhouse, a terrified Kayleigh turns to Rebecca for comfort, only to find herself developing unexplainable feelings for her new friend. Rebecca, despite her best intentions, is falling in love with Kayleigh. But when Rebecca moves in with Kayleigh to help her get to the bottom of the haunting, she finds more than she bargained for. Can Rebecca and Kayleigh overcome ghosts from the past and their own insecurities, or will a presence from the past tear them apart?

A Walk Away—Lacey Schmidt Kat and Rand's daily worlds are 2,100 miles apart, but something about their meeting on the magical shores of the nation's oldest national park east of the Mississippi sparks questions that neither woman can just walk away without answering. Sometimes chance brings you to the right person to help you resolve some of your baggage, and you learn to like yourself a little more. Kat and Rand are smart enough to recognize this chance in each other, but they also find that there is a catch to every opportunity—walking toward something is always walking away from something else.

Love Forever, Live Forever—Annette Mori No one forgets their first love. For Nicky, that's Sara, who abruptly disappears one day, leaving only a cryptic letter. That day scarred her soul. When the pain starts to diminish, Nicky begins to get her life back on track until it is derailed once again by an unimaginable twist. Changed forever, Nicky becomes a careless, womanizing nomad known as the Little Wild One, until she meets Annie. Thirteen years later, Nicky's finally settled and happy. Fate intervenes and puts her directly back into the path of her first love, Sara, and the corresponding events send her into a tailspin. Now she must decide—who will be the person she ends up living with and loving forever?

Possessing Morgan—Erica Lawson New York City, in the height of summer. Crime seems to have taken a holiday, and Detective Morgan O'Callaghan is bored, bored, bored. Paperwork is mating and multiplying on her desk, and even a jaywalker is starting to look good. Anything to get her out from behind her desk! Enter Andrea Worthington, Charleston socialite and all-around rich girl, right down to the wealthy fiancé. She's also the new Assistant District Attorney assigned to Morgan's precinct. Their first meeting is like two freight trains crashing head on. Then a high profile, career make-or-break murder case throws them together again. The investigation has barely begun when

Andrea becomes the target of a nearly fatal hit-and-run. But was it really aimed at her? Can she and Morgan find the common ground they need to solve the case and stop the attacks, or are the gaps just too wide to bridge?

Twenty-three Miles—Renee MacKenzie Talia Lisher has a long family history of lying, about anything and everything. With her father dead, and her mom gone on a quest to start a new life, Talia struggles to keep in touch with her only remaining family, her incarcerated brother. When Talia sets her sights on Officer Shay Eliot, she vows to stop lying. She starts watching Shay, waiting for just the right circumstances and amount of courage to talk to her. Talia might be watching Shay, but someone in a dark van is watching Talia. Is the mystery driver a dangerous part of her family's past, or is it all just a coincidence? Shay Eliot has left the police force because of what she perceives as a hostile work environment. When a brutal double-murder on the 23-mile-long Colonial Parkway puts the FBI's magnifying glass squarely on her, her alibi comes from an unlikely source – a young woman who has been stalking her. Shay wants to keep her distance from Talia, but once she gets to know the younger woman she can't keep feelings from developing. This is a story about community, and how it comes together in dangerous and devastating times. When you don't know who to trust, you better have friends who will rally around you. Will Talia and Shay find the answers they need to the mystery of the murders on the parkway, or will justice be elusive? Will they survive their quest for the truth?

.

E-Books, Print, Free e-books

Visit our website for more publications available online.

www.affinityebooks.com

Published by Affinity E-Book Press NZ LTD
Canterbury, New Zealand

Registered Company 2517228

www.ingramcontent.com/pod-product-compliance
Lightning Source LLC
Chambersburg PA
CBHW051243050726

47594CB00001B/284